MAHA
AVTAR

MAHA AVTAR

When the Kaliyug ENDS...

Dr. Pratyush Dhage

PARTRIDGE
A Penguin Company

**Partridge books may be ordered through booksellers or
by contacting:**

Partridge India
Penguin Books India Pvt.Ltd
11, Community Centre, Panchsheel Park, New Delhi 110017
India
www.partridgepublishing.com
Phone: 000.800.10062.62

This book is dedicated to
'My Parents,'
"Vanessa Anne Hudgens,"
&
'The Indian Railways'

PREFACE

The story in this book is a product of imagination and completely a work of fiction. If at all it reminds anybody of any incidence or person or place please consider it as a mere coincidence. The incidents in the story have been imagined from the doomsday cults which are popular in various societies the world over.

The story does not want to prove anything against anyone in particular or that something is greater than the other thing. It just wants to prove a single point that The ALMIGHTY is the single and largest force in the Universe. There might be hundreds of religions and cults in the world, there might be millions of followers of each, but in the heart of each is the belief that, "We may all call him by millions of names but all those are for the single creator and the ultimate singularity—GOD."

ACKNOWLEDGEMENTS

This is not the regular section like in the other books. I will not mention irrelevant names to just to keep people happy.

Firstly, the thing which inspired me to write this story was an animated Hindi movie called 'DASHAVTAR—The grandest animated movie ever made.' It was a 2D animation movie and the story and scale of the events in it was really mind blowing.

Secondly, I would like to thank PARTRIDGE PUBLISHING for helping me out to get my debut novel published. I had written this story in 2010-11 when I used to travel to work in the Local Trains in Mumbai. After a lot of rejections and despair it was

Evelyn Forrest from Partridge who made me go in for publishing and 'Ann' my publishing co-ordinator who helped me in further processes.

Thirdly, except my parents, no one in my friends or family knew I was writing a story and those who knew, were really not interested in it. Even in the first class compartments of the trains where I wrote this, all that I received were cold and uncomfortable stares. It was my brother 'Vishal Dhuru' who was the biggest help to me in taking my first step towards getting published. Also instrumental was my aunt Lata Dhage.

Among my friends first and foremost it was my best pal Mr. Rajan K Joshi who liked the story. Then it was Gauri Patel, Dr. Madhavi Srivastava, Dr. Siddharth Kaushal, Dr. Mamta Kaurani, Dr. Shraddha Walekar, Dr. Sadhana Sabandhasani, Dr. Sheetal Kamble and Geeta who read all or some parts of the manuscript. Though I did not get any feedback, it was very nice of them to read it.

In addition it would be thanks to all the equipment and behind the screen people who made this dream of mine to reality.

Dr. Pratyush Dhage

He was sweating a lot, even the air conditioner of the business class was proving futile to ward of his heat off. The reason—he had been rushing all the way through the airport security clearance and then to the bus for the plane. He had on the spot ticket which was 15 times the normal cost and the next flight was 20 hours later.

At an age of 23 he was the perfect example of what success meant—A perfect age, money and an exotic job and a seat in the business class. He got a window seat, sitting at the window, tears trickled from his eyes. He did not know how he was going to spend the next 18-20hours in air. The sexy flight attendant came to offer the young stud sweets but stopped when she saw the tears. Though the abuse in her profession was mind numbing, somewhere inside, she was a sensitive girl, she felt something for the crying man.

His name—Raj. As a person Raj was a thorough professional, his success had not gone into his head. The reason why he was crying was the WhatsApp message from his father which read "ur grand father is on his death bed." That moment onwards each moment reminded him of the stories his grand dad told him; all sci-fi gadgets mixed in mythology with astounding detail which only he could imagine, stories which were all alive and Raj felt inside them.

Till he got his job 1.5 years back in New York, Raj was told a story every day. A Grandson-Grandfather relation of this kind was unheard at this age, but then, so were his stories. And now the story teller was on the verge. Raj remembered how his GF really loved telling the stories of Dashavtar of Vishnu.

Over the years he told him about 9 avatars of Vishnu in full glory over and over again.

"Why don't you tell me about the 10th one?" Raj remembered asking when he was 13 years old.

"Because he has not come . . ."

"You might know when he will come . . . ???"

"No, I don't."

"Why . . . ?"

"Because no one will be left to tell the story when he comes . . ."

And Raj was all quiet when he used to hear that.

One day his GF said to him, "You know what the best thing about the 10th avatar is?"

"What?" Raj asked big eyes.

"No one knows when he will come, where he will come. Everyone just knows why he will come . . ." Raj was lost and speechless.

"Nobody has thought but I will tell you a story which will describe this all, in a way we both love it."

"With, gadgets and all that???"

"Yes . . . ." Raj noticed the lively sparkle and glint in his Grandfather's eye.

"Start from tomorrow . . ."

"No no . . ."

"Why?"

"Do you know what the 10th Avatar is?"

"Yes, it's KALKI . . ."

"No, it's not that simple. When you say Dashavtar, it is the grand culmination of what God is. It is when the Almighty takes the last step to rid the earth of unholiness. The 10th avatar is unimaginable power which holds the universe together, the ultimate expression of God and his power. It is the Avatar which all gods wait with a bated breath, the final answer to every question on the planet."

"Wow . . ."

"He will be the biggest and the largest force, the massiveness of the whole universe at a single point, he will be the phenomena of a millions of years, and he is what will be wilder than the wildest imagination ever. For the evil shall never be prepared for the grandest reply of Godliness"

Raj was all over the moon.

"Do you know the designation of the 10th one?"

"What?"

"He is the MAHA-AVATAR."

"I will wait for it . . . the story."

"May be it will be the last story I will tell you . . ." And Raj hugged his grand dad tight with tears in his eyes.

The plane teared through the air at 800kmph, below was the vast expanse of the Atlantic which he could not see. Then he fell asleep. The air hostess pulled a blanket over him and lovingly moved her hand in his silky smooth hair. After a sleep of 4 hours, he woke up in cold sweat, removed his blanket and gulped down a full bottle of water. He looked around; no one was awake except for the air hostess. He looked out of the window; the glowing lights of the cities which he saw were a reminder of the stories, Surreal. Suddenly his heart skipped a beat as he saw a shadow approach him. It was the air hostess.

"Are you fine Raj?" She asked.

"How do you know my name?"

"I read the boarding list, but that's not important; are you fine?"

"Kind of no, can you switch on the lights?"

"I am sorry sir, it will irk the others; may I walk you to the bar instead?"

"Ok fine."

The bar was the only place where the lights were on. He was still uncomfortable on the bar stool. She asked if he needed some drink, to which he replied "Lemonade."

"Excuse me?"

"Lime juice it means . . ." Raj replied.

"Actually sir no one asks for non alcoholic beverages here, so I thought I heard it wrong." She replied.

"Yes, I understand, but I don't like alcohol." He thought and said as she handed him a fresh lime juice. He felt better after drinking it and soothed down a little.

"What's your name?" he asked her.

"Lina." She replied and then weirdly looked at her golden nameplate. Then as he sipped the juice she looked at him, at the base of her heart, she felt nice that he did not drink.

"Why are you so worried?" She asked.

"My GF is on death bed." He replied. Lina scratched her brain, GF for her was girlfriend.

"What happened to her?"

"Her??? He's my grandfather."

"Oh!" she replied, then added; "You know even I am close to mine, but he did not like me being an air hostess."

"Can we talk about something else Lina?" She felt a tingle as he spoke her name. They talked about other things, and as Lina was, she managed to keep his mind away from his thoughts in a light way.

3 Hours later—"Sir, do have a nap now, you will need to be energetic tomorrow." Raj was feeling sleepy; he went back to his recliner seat and lied down. Lina pulled a blanket on him. The next day the plane landed at the Santacruz International Airport, Mumbai.

As Raj walked down the artificial tunnel and health scans, he met Lina. Even though he was tenser than ever, he stopped when he saw her, to say thanks, and then before she could say anything, moved ahead quickly.

"We will meet again, hopefully." He was gone by the time she said that.

3 hours later Raj was in the hospital. His dad was waiting for him. He felt proud to see his successful son.

"Where is he?" Raj asked shaking like a leaf.

"Inside VVIP ward, private room number 10." The number pierced his heart. He saw his GF, all frail and weak on the bed and that moment he broke down completely as he held the near lifeless hand of his GF.

"Why do we become so helpless in hospitals?" he squeaked as he cried. "I hate hospitals and I hate doctors." Tears fell on his GF's hand.

Half an hour later, his father entered and gave him a leather bound diary. It had a lock on it which went right through the pages of the diary at 3 places.

"Where's the key?" Raj asked expectantly.

"Papa said that you would know where to search for it." Raj's father said.

Raj gave his brain a run thinking for a place and then, "Where is his mobile?"

"At home, why?" His father answered and asked.

"Please tell someone to bring it."

"Sure, now you get fresh, here is a set of clothes; your mom will get some food and the mobile for you. Now go." Raj father said.

2 hours later Raj's mom came with a meal and mobile. A tight hug was what she gave Raj first of all. "Love you mom." Raj said

She laid out the meal and asked Raj to have it. "Give me the mobile first."

"Eat first." His mom said in the 'mummy stern tone.' And Raj had his super spicy Indian meal. After 3 years of bland food in New York, his tongue and teeth welcomed the best cuisine in the world by gorging on it.

After the meal, he quickly took the mobile phone and switched it off. He then took of the back cover. In between the back cover and the SIM card was an empty space, 10*7*6 millimetres in dimensions. In that small cave was a broken key, until the shank.

Dr. Pratyush Dhage

His father saw it in astonishment and said 'wow' to himself. "But how will you turn it?" He questioned.

"Where is his shaving kit?" Raj asked.

His father took out the small bag from the small cupboard near the bed and asked, "Here, but what will you do with it?"

"Just a minute . . ." Raj muttered, as he opened the box and scanned it for something. "Yesss." He said slowly as he found what he was searching for; a square tipped pair of tweezers. His mom squinted one eye as she saw her son meddle around with unrelated things.

Raj picked up the broken key by the shank with the tweezers, and then he slid the key in the key hole/slot of the diary. Then with a firm grip of the tweezers he twisted the shank and, with a click the lock was open.

Raj's father was amazed over what he saw. It made him well up and be proud at the same time.

"It's time we leave him alone." He said to his wife.

Raj opened the diary, the title page read . . .

MAHA-AVTAR

BLUECOVER Corp.

It was a large scale of buildings, below the level and heights of a 2 storey building; standing on and beside a river near its source.

Unlike most rivers, this one has its origin in 2 very large springs, in the most remote inaccessible jungle in India. A portion of the spring gives out scalding hot water and the other just 2 meters away gives out icy cold water. Why this occurs is unknown . . .

This location was discovered in 1985 during an expedition for the discovery of a new botanical species. Before the expeditions could come to any fruitful result, all the botanical experts died.

A month later a defence expedition was sent in which found the 13 bodies of the experts below a feet of cold water. The bodies were taken back and investigations were carried out. They could only prove that the hands and feet were mangled. No sign of attempted murder or poisoning was there. When all the investigations turned null, the bodies were cryo-transported to the Occult-Study Faculty, U.S.S.R. There an intelligent guy suggested Bone Scans. 5 days later this decision gave fruit.

The scan showed long bone involvement to the max. But the surprise was the SYMMETRIC involvement of those 12 bones.

The person who made the discovery was a senior good-named doc of the institute. He wanted to make the cases public in journals and news. He was found dead in cryopreservation 2 days later.

The bodies were brought back to India and cremated in presence of defence officials and relatives. 15 days later the people involved in the 2nd expedition met with the same fate. Not to be deterred, the government sent inside one more funded expedition which never came back. This filled terror in the minds of the officials. There was no use sending more people in the jungle. It had become a force to reckon with. Hence they quarantined the whole jungle and performed a cover up. Since the media was not far reached those days no one knew about the incidents.

15 years later, the times changed. In 2000 A.D., the defence wing gave the contract of the state of the art research faculty to be built in that region to a Russian company. In mid 2000 hence, the Bluecover Labs were established. All those who were a help in the construction and setup were killed by a series of incidents in Russia. Even the Prime Minister or the President did not have any info regarding the whereabouts of the Labs.

Keeping the Labs undercover was comparatively easy for the Defence wings. There was an opaque forest cover over it, so it was not visible in satellite imaging, and Russian defence grade jammers cut out even defence positioning signals in the complete region.

Bluecover Corp Labs had a self monitored CDMA Hotlink Network. All employees had special cell phones which were usable only in the Lab premises. If by chance the cell-phone was smuggled out and switched on, its software was programmed to self destruct in 1 second on coming in contact with any GSM, CDMA, TDMA, Wi-Fi, WI-MAX network or even AM-Radio signal. It could only be connected to a BlueC-OS on PC otherwise in 1 second it was just a piece of useless circuits. Only for top level officials and employees on mission could the cell phone be taken out.

The corporation carried out many activities like acquiring land, closed large scale buildings, encounters etc. However, it was so stealth in doing that no one ever knew who was behind all this even the people working there did not know that many of the incidents countrywide were put to effect by them. The ones who tried to get extra were invariably never seen again.

Bluecover had a very modern system of transport. Modern system means a technology which was futuristically ahead of time. Invisibility is a boon that humanity desires and Bluecover believed in getting such things to reality. The road reaching Bluecover was a 4 lane concrete one at a height of 100Ft. The road was reached by taking a 14km long underground detour from the new National Highway to join the old. To the public however, the old National Highway was closed. On the old highway after going 40kms there was another detour which after going a further 10kms had a dead end at a gorge. This is where the super tech started. Bluecover had a technology by which an image behind an opaque object could be displayed on its front, so when in real life, the object could only viewed with the image projection off. When the projection was switched on all one could see was the projected image and not the object, making it 'Invisible' to the eye. Bluecover Corp had used this tech in its vehicles and on the opaque cover on the bridge which was required to cross the gorge to reach the Labs. This was the single reason that for the naked eye the gorge was the end of the road, but when the tech was switched off, it was the entry to the most advanced research labs of the world. The road from the gorge climbed to a height of 100Ft in a continuous turn, the road was wide enough to let the car climb at speeds of until 150kmph. Next, to prevent the shadow from sunlight, there had been installed multiple sources of daylight illumination beneath the bridge. This ensured that the shadow of the bridge never appeared in photographs. The illuminators had sensors which adjusted the illumination according to the sun's brightness and angle.

Bluecover had the tech in many modes to the bridge. The aerial view was permanently switched on, so in satellite imaging it was invisible. When the specialized cars let out a code at the gorge, the projection was switched off for a period of 10seconds. This was to allow the vehicle to gain a proper entry onto the gradient road. As the vehicle proceeded ahead on the road, the tech was switched off in a sectional sequence. It appeared as if the road was disappearing as the vehicle surged forward. No stopping was allowed at or on the bridge. To avoid the problems of tyre bursts a variant of maglev technology was used to propel the vehicles to super speeds. When on the gradient road section, two bearings would come out from the side of the vehicle and get aligned with one of the side wall of the bridge which would hold the vehicle in a straight as the magnetic levitation would be activated. A very secret organisation had been entrusted to do the work. And after the construction the workers and engineers were completely isolated in the labs. They were never allowed to leave. This was to prevent the breach of any information of the location of the labs to the outside world.

Next were the ID's of the employees. The format of the id changed along with the rank status of the employee. It ranged from a simple finger print activated card to a holograph focussing device for the top officials. The former was a better developed version of the usual biometric system. When in the normal system only one finger sufficed, here the person had to place one thumb on the scanner and slide the card in a slot. When the card was in place in the slot, it too acted as a scanner. When the database verified the 3 similar prints of the 2 thumbs and the index finger, the person was allowed entry.

———∞∞∞———

Present Day, at an unrelated place-

The clouds of college life still hang over my head, whenever I feel sad or pathetic they rain and refresh me up again.

Now it was Anvesha's time to end college and to enjoy the rain later when she needed it the most.

I'm there to meet her; she's cleared her 4th year and is coming for a vacation, so it's party time for me, Anvesha and her group. Its months since I've hugged my darling. Just to come early, she's in a train from NDLS. I don't remember the name exactly but its arrival in here is 10:30 AM.

Hey' the train's come . . . Love you Anvi . . .

The magnificent train chugged into the station. The A/C 2 tier boggie had an exact place where I was. Even before the train slowed down, "My sweetheart Yash . . ." I heard the world's 2nd sweetest voice shouting from the boggie door.

"I'm going to jump!" She shouted.

"No, let the train stop." I threw a very caring dialogue, which met deaf ears. When the train was slow enough she jumped into my arms. Many people saw it. Some admired, some made faces, one girl clapped.

"Yash sir missed you a lot!" And Anvesha hugged me very tightly.

"Love you a lot lot lot!" I chipped and let her down.

'12 months since I saw you darling!" She rubbed her nose on mine and said.

"Make it short Sweetie, say 1 year!" she giggled. Anvesha looked divine when she laughed. She felt so lovely to talk to and take in arms. I was the luckiest guy on earth to have a fiancée like her.

"You know Yash; I'm going to do my internship here!" She happily chirped.

"Well then, my darling's here only." I ruffled her hair.

"Come let's go inside . . ." She pulled me inside the train. "Anvi, the train will leave."

"5 Minutes is a loooooooooooong time train boy." And she was successful in persuading me. Inside the train, she talked without brakes and laughed along . . . breathing along when she remembered.

The train jerked. "Let me go." I said getting up from the berth.

"Nooooo, you are not going anywhere now!" Anvesha had a big laugh and hugged me. I ran to the door, the train had paced up but I could get off it. I was about to do so when . . .

"Hey you'll break your bones if you jump!" Anvi shouted and pulled me back. The speed was same at which she had jumped. "But you jumped at the same speed!" I protested.

"But you were there to hold me naa!" She said very very cutely, bringing her lower lip over her upper. We went back to the berth and a chat ensued.

"Good, now for the whole day you are with me."

"So darling, now what do you feel?"

"Cool, I'll have double the fun you had!" Anvi chipped.

"Miss cute, I'll be in trouble if the TT finds out!" I said worried.

"Don't worry sir, he won't say a word!"

"Don't say sir from now on! You and I are the same now." And Anvi nodded a Yes!

"You know Yash; I'll go to the college in the morning and to your clinic in the evening."

"Well many boys will be after you in the new college . . ."

"I've this for them sir . . . oops Yash!" and I got to see her taser.

"Well, no tension then . . ." I hushed.

The train was nearing its final destination.

"Avnika's on the station Yash, and good that you are also with me. I've a lot of luggage . . ." Anvi said as her bag count reached nine.

"So that's why you stopped me!" I said picking up a rucksack.

"Don't you dare touch a bag!" she said angrily.

"I did not mean it that way . . ."

"You can hold this if you want to help" she handed me her handbag and laughed. Err . . . giggled.

'Help . . .' I said to myself. The train stopped. Anvi hopped down, a coolie rushed to take down her luggage and she did not let me lift anything except her handbag. Minutes later, she and her best friend Avnika had 'that' hugging programme.

"Hey I did not know that he also had a booking!" Avni asked surprised.

"Ha ha! He did not have any booking; I did not let him get down . . ." Anvi chuckled and they both had a funny laugh.

The coolie lugged the luggage on the trolley. We walked to the parking and I still had the handbag. Outside gleaming in the sun was Anvi's dark violet Lancer. It now had 3 spoke alloys like Avni's Car. "Yeyyyyy . . . . !" Anvesha shouted as she unlocked the boot with her remote.

"Yash sir you drive!" she handed me the keys. Avni took to the back seat, and Anvi gave directions. She seemed to know all the roads with minimal traffic and signals.

"Hey Anvesha, your parents are out for a week." Avni said.

"Then I'll drop my luggage and come over to your place." Anvesha gave a solution, and Avni's eyes had a definite sparkle on that. I saw it in the rear view mirror. We dropped the luggage at Anvi's home and went to Avnika's. On the way we passed the Science Institute.

"Hey doc's, that's where I did my Masters . . ." I remembered Avnika's research during studies. I did not know what subjects she studied but she was definitely more qualified than us two.

We reached her high-tech house. It was in one of the most isolated locality of the city. Also, it did not like a girl's room at all. I mean I saw a shelf, No a huge shelf (It was around 3 times a normal bed) stacked to the grill with books, and no they were no magazines or funny jokes but Genetics, Forensic medicine, genetic medicine, Microforensics . . . etc etc. I could not even read the names of many in the first go.

She showed us around the house.

One room was a guest room with a neatly laid out bed.

The second one was what she called her Relaxing Room . . . it had a 82 inch LED-TV, a Blu-Ray Player, a 9.2 surround sound system and LED relax illumination. I could imagine easily as to why it was her relaxing room . . .

She was reluctant to show us the other room and when I saw it . . . I knew why, it was her study room. As I stepped into the room, I saw a table and chair, which were the only things in place in the room. Rest were hundreds of books scattered among thousands of papers. All had DNA patterns, codes of A-G-C-T strands, chemical equations, and organic chemistry concepts scribbled on them. The wall had a white paint and Avnika was approx 5'8 in height, she had completely scribbled the walls with her study concepts till a height of 6'2.

"Actually I get too much involved in study so I write on whatever I get at hand." Avnika said with a sheepish smile. She said that jokingly but I could only imagine her when she would in that study mood.

"Anvesha, you can freshen up and pick any outfit you want." Avni said.

Anvesha did not stop to listen more and she closed the door.

Avni and I came into the drawing room. "Tell me, what exactly do you research in?"

"I do genome mapping." She replied

"And you are qualified in . . . ?"

"I'm a PhD in Forensic Genetics . . ." I could only admire her study level.

"You must be paid handsomely isn't it?" I asked casually.

"Mmmm . . . 25.2 . . ." she replied coolly.

"What 25.2?" I blankly asked.

"Lakhs per month . . ." she said and I sprang 4 feet in the air. That salary (if you could call that a salary) easily explained her super modified car and lifestyle.

Anvesha came out of the room.

"Excuse me!" Avnika picked a towel and went into the same room.

Anvesha sat by my side, and held my hand. I looked at her and then into her eyes.

"Finally you are with me!" I squeezed her hand and said. Her reaction to that resembled the Purring of a cat. Her hair were still wet, hand was super soft, lips were coral pink and the way she bit her lower lip was an expression worth MILLIONS . . .

"You know Yash; it was kind of strange without you these 3 years. 12 guys proposed me but I missed you all the time, and when my dad suggested . . . ." Anvi stopped.

"What happened?"

"I talk too much . . ."

There was nobody around, we were just 2 alone. The situation was too romantic but it seemed funny a few seconds later coz we were only sitting and looking at each other. I don't know what she found looking at a crank like me but I was looking at a mischievous beauty. A minute later, we burst out laughing.

Avni was ready with the lunch, joking along we had it.

"Time to go miss!" I said after the meal.

"I pulled you along, so I'll drop you back." Anvesha said.

"Hey, then take my car! It's not been driven for a month!" Saying this Avni threw the keys to Anvesha.

"Not driven for a month?" I was surprised, "How come?"

"I'll tell that later!" Anvesha also picked up the flat keys.

We reached the basement to the car. Avni had 9-10 cars including some high end ones, but she loved modifying her Swift, it was this one which she never gave anyone else other than Anvesha to drive. It was a white one with black and white bumpers and weird designs all over it, along with fog lamps in the bumper. The headlights were projector type, as an extravagance it even had projector reverse lights, a wide focus tail light, a rear spoiler with working taillights, 3 spoke deep center alloy wheels, a sun roof, 3 top shelf tuning kits in the engine, 4 scissor doors, blue tinted windshields and windows, even a working air intake on the bonnet and finally an exorbitant complete neon system in side and below the car. It resembled one of those amazing and illegal streetcars.

"Yash, she's on a task for a month and its taking a very long time to map out a genome sequence, she sits at it for over 9 hours every evening and she's only 70% done." Anvesha said as she squealed the tyres.

"Oh!" I said quietly, 25.2 Lakhs per month would require talent and perfection by the quintals.

"She's in the study room by now and that's why I came with you!" Anvi said as the Speedo needle reached 145kmph on the highway road. Compared to Avnika's study, we were still in Playgroup.

She stopped the car at an open stretch of road. "What happened?"

"Nothing." She replied and stepped out. It was monsoon, so the highway surroundings were lush green. She came by my side, stood close and leaned on my shoulder.

Nobody of us spoke a word. 5 minutes later she planted 2 deep kisses on my neck. "Hey hey!" I exclaimed. She shyly blushed and went back to the driver's seat. I could not get what came over her but she was red-faced till we reached my house.

"You are coming inside!" I said as she neared my house.

"No please, not now!" she said shyly.

"Pleeeease . . . ." I requested.

"No, Yash! My hair are open!"

"That's the lamest excuse I've ever heard." I giggled. "But as you wish!" I added.

It was nearly dark-dusky, but as soon as she opened the doors of the car, every eye turned towards it.

Scissor doors are only seen in games in 99% of India. Here, it was as real as a carious tooth. 10 minutes later, she left. Those blinking neon's dazzled all the pairs of eyes looking at the car and her. Anvesha anyways, had a habit of switching on, each and every neon of her Car, so anybody who was not interested in cars was also forced to look at it. At present, Avnika's Car had plethora of them so every head turned.

Well, Anvesha made an event out of a small incident of meeting her, but it felt lovely, especially that kiss. My mom asked as to why I did not bring the cute girl inside, I made up a silly answer and went to the clinic.

A few days passed. All TV channels and bearded saints on them were proclaiming it as the most vulnerable time of mankind. A different thing altogether.

On a Sunday, Anvi called me. "Hey Yash, clinic open today?"

"No! Why?"

"I'll come every Sunday, don't close it from now on!"

"But Sweetie, don't you need rest?"

"Yash, I've not started intern yet! And being with you relaxes me to the maxxxx!!"

"Ok then come home, we'll go together!"

"Hey, you know! I've now got front scissor doors on my Car too!" Well, my place had something new to see now. 1 hour later, I saw the Dark Violet Lancer and Anvesha stepped out in a dark violet suit. Take my word . . . SHE LOOKED AWESOME . . . I 'Hiiiii'ed her from the window and she opened all the 4 doors of her car. It looked straight out of an Auto-Show. I called her in.

She had her hair tied up that day and 2 cute earrings. My mom was very happy over me having such a lovely friend. She had already made coffee for Anvi . . . I was required to make my cup on my own. 10 minutes later we walked towards the clinic. I opened the lock and she pushed the door open.

"Don't expect many patients today!" I said. She had her apron on by that time, and looked even lovelier with it. Many a times I thought that she deserved someone much better than me . . .

Minutes later a lady walked in with a child directly to Anvi. She looked as if she had hurried up the morning.

"Doctor, can you help me?" the lady said. "Sure, what seems to be the problem?" I asked.

"Actually doc . . . , we are working parents and return late; my mother takes care of her! She said that Nishka's teeth need filling!" Anvesha lifted up the 4 yr old girl. The girl showed her teeth to her as "EEEEEE . . ." and giggled. "No problem, we'll see that mommy doesn't have any problem now!" Anvi said to Nishka as she placed the kid on the dental chair.

She put some talcum powder on the gloves so that Nishka felt good when she placed the gloved hands near her mouth. Very delicately she examined and proceeded to place the airmotor in her mouth. There was no need to hurry up, and hurrying up with children is equal to being a 'Devil at work'. Even for once did I hear any 'oooo' or 'aaa' from the kid! When Anvi placed the motor on the teeth, she asked me to play a kids song on the cell phone.

Fortunately, I had one. The song depressed the sound of the instrument and Nishka was at ease. She had decayed left upper and lower back teeth so it was a single sitting affair.

While leaving, the lady said, "God bless you both!" I felt warm inside, Anvi blushed and looked gorgeous.

"Will you come every Sunday?" I asked her.

"Yes . . . . promise." She said squeezing my hand. "Ok then!" We sat for 2-3 hours. A few unexpected patients came and she did the work better than me.

After she left, I ordered a special board stating her name on it in bold letters, which was a visual treat, just like her. The next Sunday when Anvesha saw it she was on cloud 9. My mom was double minded over the incident but was happy have my beautiful friend at our house, now every week.

"Why don't you keep her here for the rest of your life?" My mom asked me a question, which caused an adrenaline release in my body. Well, life had a beautiful pace. I did not expect anything weird to take place. Anvesha started her internship. The first day itself she received 3 proposals and very rudely she rejected them.

On a Sunday like other ones, we were at a bite spot and Anvi had something interesting to tell . . .

"Yash, Avni completed the genome mapping. It took her over 6 months. Normally it takes her only 2 months."

"Why so long this time?"

"Don't know!"

"It might have taken a hell lot of time, to do that?"

"Nooo, thanks to Anik!" Anvi said with a triumph feel.

"Is your this friend in the same field?" I asked.

"No way, he works as a software developer for some very big company; He had made specialized software which had all the genome maps."

'Another super intelligent guy!' I thought.

"He gets 10.5 per month only but leads a more peaceful life than Avnika." Anvesha hushed finally. "Oh!"

"You know, Anik can be a great hacker if he wants!" Anvi giggled. We had a coffee at my house and then she left.

I was watching TV. Nothing special was going on so I was surfing senselessly. A headline caught my attention.

'2 die of cancer.' I thought, 'Media has lost subjects for making news, once they blew the H1N1 thing out of proportion.' However, I continued to watch the news. They were showing the bone scans. It showed that the tumour had metastasised to all the 12 long bones of the body—Symmetrically.

'Well that's exactly nothing to make news of!' I thought and picked up the remote to change the channel, when, 'Abhi channel mat badaliyega . . .' the reporter said. I looked here and there. That line took me by surprise. They showed the 2nd patients bone scans. It too showed the same 12 bone involvement—Symmetrically.

It was one of the freakiest happenings in medical co-incidence. This thing could make good news. Nearly every channel was showing this same news. One case was in Mumbai and the other in Kolkata. Days passed, people forgot all about the co incidence.

Some 15 days later the TV was choc a bloc with a spate of 200 deaths due to bone cancer in a span of a month, and the common things were the 12 bone symmetric involvement and all these were criminals in jails all over India, people were happy over it in a weird manner.

On a detailed analysis of the first two cases, it was brought to notice that those two were involved with some research and had met each other a few days ago. Now this info had only a little significance for medico-investigation except the occupation. 'Tumours are not communicable' was the binding answer.

What seemed like a freak incident was being hailed as a planned invasion now. Sadhus and others hailed it as the 'Vishwa Ka Anth.' Muslims were like 'Qayamat Ka Din,' and finally Christians awaited the 'Judgement Day!' everything this way or the other proclaimed it as the arrival of the end of the earth. It was a topic which had taken to the parliament.

"What are the reasons for these deaths?" was the only question in the question hour for the past few weeks, and no one had any answer. Something was really wrong somewhere. Some made fun, some flouted the news . . . one thing was for sure, there was fear in everybody's mind.

Few days later it was time to for me to buy my own car, and it was not a simple decision to come to . . . following were the reasons-

1. "Put as much money as you can and buy the latest model" said one.
2. "No use, the world is coming to an end! Save the money."
3. "Take a very costly one on loan, if the world ends you won't have to pay it back." was one of the most given advice.

I had my eyes set on a car, which could go dirty in the outland with ease. Anvesha was in her car when we had a small chat.

"You know, I always dreamt of buying a GYPSY and modifying it!" I said. She pulled me close to her and started her car. Then she gave a peck on my cheek, winked at me and said,

"Modifying is my job!"

10-12 days later we both were at a showroom where the dealer had a GYPSY for us. "Plain grey colour sir . . . for any other colour you will have to wait for 9 months, no one orders this model nowadays."

"9 months???? Man you can get a baby in that time." I said and Anvesha smirked.

"Then treat your new car as a baby." The sales guy said. I did not want to reply to that. I did not want the colour but waiting for months made me go for it.

"So when do you want a party?"

"Did I ask for it?" She asked in a childish tone.

"No . . . . but still?"

"When you take your car home, that time you give one big one!"

"Eh??"

"You are taking my car home. Next week I'll bring a double new GYPSY to you." And she gave me her car keys.

The kids around my place were waiting for me at home. They were excited about the car more than me. There excitement dipped when they saw a long car but it returned when they saw the scissor doors on the car. I tried my level best to keep off their fiddly fingers from the dash.

A week later Anvi brought my Pearlescent Dark Violet GYPSY and it sure looked stunning. She showed me all the modifications and needless to say it was my dream come true. The kids came running out and we all went for a long ride in the new car. It was a different feeling driving my own car. Then the next day was a party. Anvi came with her hi-fi friends and we had a peacefully rocking time at my house. After the dinner we went out for a walk. Anik and Kelly took to their own, Avni was on a phone call and Anvesha and I had our love and geek talks.

Avni came towards us. "Hey docs can I leave?"

"Why what happened?" Anvi popped.

"Work yaar, nothing else. Will have to go to the office, just got a call. The vehicle will be here in 25 minutes. You all continue . . . ok." And she walked out.

———— ∞∞∞ ————

She got into the car. Each time she would think that why could she not see the car until it came very close to her?

The door of the car was raised to let her in. She stepped inside and the door closed automatically. The display in front of her came to life and the destination blinked in a weird purple colour. The 2nd display showed the path ahead as 10 headlights of the car illuminated the road.

Bluecover was so flawless in all its activities, be it in the labs with the super technology she had at her disposal or with the way in which she was picked up from wherever she was.

The car showed the right turn indicator and all of the sudden the road ahead went dark. The headlights had been switched off.

The turn literally went on for a few minutes. This was a place which she could never imagine about where it was. Of all the places she had travelled, never had she encountered or felt a turn which would last for a few minutes. She knocked on the opaque partition which separated the passenger from the driver. "Switch on the lights." she said but the driver did not respond.

2 minutes later, the display showed some light and the car stopped turning into infinity. She closed her eyes to get over that turning feeling.

When she opened her eyes again the display was all alive. The road visibility was akin a summer afternoon and the road was straight ahead into ecstasy.

The car speedometer reading forwarded from 150kmph to 275kmph in a minute and stabilized at that position.

The first display showed

'Arrived at main destination, enter sub-destination'

Avnika tapped on the 'Microforensic Research' on the map. Both the displays went blank and after 3 more turns, the car stopped and the door popped open. 'MICROFORENSIC RESEARCH' the name welcomed her as she stepped out. In a second she turned around but the car had disappeared.

Location—Bluecover Corp.

The labs were a place of premier and hardening research. However, it was not a place where things could go on any one persons wish ignoring the others. Therefore any big event was required to be passed by the 25 most important people in the Bluecover Corp. These 25 people were required to place their palms on the electronic chronicle in The

Dome to register the event. Then a code would be released for the event and associated actions.

For the past years, research had been going on to find the causes for the very horrible and mysterious deaths in the region. After a yearlong of testing and many deaths later it was found that the water was the causative agent. To prevent those, too frequent test related deaths, Blue cover Labs resorted to using Hover cycles for every movement outside the building. Chemical analysis of the water could only prove '0'. Researchers at the faculty were at a complete loss as to how the water was causing deaths so torturous and blazingly fast. Then a biological analysis of the water showed some result which excited all. The hot water showed many organisms, but they were all primitive heat and cold resistant bacteria which were known since ages and it was back to square one each time.

The labs proposed to setup a different wing for weapon research, disappointed by the failures the proposal was not met with much enthusiasm. Then, entered in the scene the defence spokesperson of India—Sheemal Jezebeth. Just like the name he had, he carried an evil face. With the entire high source, he managed to pass the proposal for the new Cybernetic Division of the Bluecover Corp.

This was a new field in India, not much research was carried initially but within a period of 6 months it picked up. In order to develop high profile war and civil defence arsenal, the labs had shifted its focus to innocent looking objects such as everyday gadgets. Bluecover Corp. was trying to convert things such as cell phones, televisions, pens, music players and specially cameras in to sophisticated human eliminating devices.

One would be hard pressed to imagine how a music player would kill a person but the research in this field had been successful. Regardless of the form, all of those devices had a few things in common which were,

1. Surface finger print scanners,
2. Tracing Circuit,
3. Iris Diameter Scanners, and most importantly
4. EDA. Acronym for Eliminating Device Activator.

This EDA was the second biggest achievement of the cybernetic division after the Teleporting Technology. It was manually controlled. Initially these devices depended on the defence database to carry out commands and could do nothing if the scan results were not present in the database. In the future these devices were enriched, with another unique circuit, 'Position Locator'. This circuit could locate the device to +-10cm's accuracy. It had its own system of positioning. It gave the Latitude-Longitude along with 10 reference points.

2 years later the labs created a technology for cameras. They created the zoom lens in 2 slices

and between the 2 slices they placed a 'Subject Positioner'. This unique circuit could locate with satellites the location of the person being photographed. Once the subject identity was updated in the database it could be tracked, LIVE. The second lens of the zoom system was also prepared in 2 slices by Kris, a junior researcher of the labs. Between those 2 slices he placed a self activated ED circuit, which he timed to 3 days. This EDA by passed the need of confirming or the manual release of any command for confirmation of the subject elimination. These lenses when incorporated in the camera gave a completely new meaning to SHOOT AT SIGHT. Kris was ecstatic over this the invention of his. He directly went to Sheemal Jezebeth, the whole and sole of the Cybernetic division to show his work.

The boss feigned disinterest with the work, however, he took the device to his house and connected the device to his work station and reset the timer to 2 minutes. Now he had to test the death device. He saw his servant sleeping outside with his face towards the pedestal fan. SJ zoomed up to the latter's face and clicked a photo. The camera then showed the next on its display for the next minute;

<SAVING–PERFORMING OPTIMIZED SUBJECT IDENTIFICATION SCAN–LOCATING SUBJECT POSITION–ACCESSING DATABASE–UPDATING DATABASE–VERIFYING SUBJECT POSITION– ACQUIRING NEAREST ASSAULT DEVICE

STATUS–DISABLING ASSAULT DEVICE CONNECTIONS–RESETTING ASSAULT DEVICE–PROCESSING ED–ED ACTIVE–TARGET LOCKED–ELIMINATION BEGINS IN 30 SECONDS>

SJ strained his eyes in the dark but he could get only a faint glimpse. He switched on the outside LED. It was clear now.

30 seconds later the fan started making noise which woke up the servant. He rubbed his eyes and looked at the LED and then at the fan. It was now making a racket. The front lid had fallen off. The servant pressed the button to switch off the fan but it did not stop. The fan was rotating at the max speed now. In a flash second the blades came off the motor and slit the throat of the man who dropped dead.

The display of the camera showed TARGET ELIMINATED . . . SJ gave an evil laugh and slept. He had a gem of device in his hands. The next day before giving the device back SJ reverted back the original settings with a tweak. However he did not appreciate the work done. Kris was not at all satisfied by the reaction of his senior. Sitting at his workplace he planned to do the unthinkable, smuggling the camera out of Bluecover and testing it . . .

He stealthily placed the camera in a commercial camera counter of a very big and established super electronics store. Back home, he tracked the device.

1. It was a rainy day, a boy and girl sat under a bus stand shelter having so called mushy talks. A photographer sitting in the stand opposite to them took out his new 400X super zoom camera, zoomed up to their face's and found the couple to be better than average. He clicked a total of 20 snaps and then selected the best one for his news paper. The next day the couple was on the front page of the news paper under the title—LOVE IN THE RAIN.

   The boy and girl were the face of the city; they took a leave from their jobs for the day and enjoyed the day. Wherever they went they heard "Hey the couple in the paper," "Rainy Lovebirds." In short all the good lines which anyone would get when printed for a good reason.

   3 Days later—The couple was printed in a different paper, but this time—they were dead. Their faces were scarred, pitted and displayed the signs of leprosy like ailment. Nobody knew what happened to them.

   The photographer was an experienced one, but this was the freakiest incident in his 35 year career. Till now he had snapped many big-wigs but never had such a thing happened. However, this incident slipped from his mind.

2. The photographer was assigned a job of taking spy pictures of a famous Hollywood actress

who was visiting India for the first time. He went around his job and got some of the most unbelievable close ups of the beauty which pleased the editor and doubled the circulation of the newspaper. The newspaper made him the head leader of his workplace and gave him a substantial raise. The next day the actress checked out of the hotel and went further with her multi country visit, next, to The USA and checked in at a hotel.

2 days later—The actress was living on the 100th floor of a hotel. It was her date to leave the country. At 0500hrs she, her secretary and 4 bodyguards got into the lift and touched the '0' floor button. At the 97th floor the lift cable snapped . . .

To prevent all the negative publicity, the hotel performed a massive cover up. The news never came out in the real form.

Back in India, the photographer was enjoying a new life. He had bought a new farm house for fulfilling his dream of living in a bungalow. On the way he snapped over 200 photographs of nature, animals, the sunset, the sunrise etc. Unknown to his knowledge however, by sheer chance the lens also captured a Shepard.

3 days later—He went in to the village and roamed in it completely, double checked each and every lane. He was happy to find that there was no casualty. The ghost of the couple still haunted a big portion of his brain. He returned home a happy man thinking that it was only a dirty game of fate.

His new house was completely set up now; he had called family and friends for the party. As was expected the party rocked the neighbourhood and everyone had a blast. At around 2330hrs the party ended. His son, a lad of 15 years, was surprised at the fact that his dad did not click any pictures at the party with his new snapper. He went to his dad's cupboard and found the new classy camera among the many models kept there. When everyone (i.e. dad, mom and little sis) was in the bedroom he kept the camera on the table and set the timer at 10 seconds. The exact time was 23:59:55 when he set the timer. He jumped on to the bed pointed a finger to the camera and shouted, "Look there and smile!" everyone looked at the camera and did the same. The photograph was clicked at 00:00:05.

The photographer looked at the camera in horror when he identified the instrument . . . did his son seal everyone's fate? He was exhausted and dropped asleep.

2 days later—While returning from work, he found the village mourning over the death of the headman. He saw the headman's photo beside the body. His body and his tractor were found in the village pond. His body was all hard and puffed up and he died 2 days back. The photographer was devastated; he rushed back to his home, took out his camera and scrolled down all the photos but could not find the head man in any of the photos.

At around 2350hrs he woke up in horror in a nightmare and drank a full bottle of water and ran to the table where the camera was still lying. Sweating profusely he glanced through the photos once again and this time he saw a head poking in one of the landscape photographs. He zoomed in the photo up to the face and recognised it as the Headman. With trembling fingers he scrolled and tried to delete the family photo. The display however showed 'ED Active'. He tried to find the memory card slot, but he forgot that the device only had internal memory.

He smelt something, a gas leak. He rushed to the kitchen; it was stinking with Ethyl Mercaptan. He went to the cylinder closet and saw the 3 cylinders with the slit pipe near the broken food processor which was still running. In fearful haste his fingers went to switch off the food processor. With a spark the button switched off and the next moment a violent blast turned him to smithereens. The blast shook the house and took away half of it. The short circuit reached the air conditioner and there was another blast, this time in the compressor, which in turn dislodged the AC from its holding in the wall and it fell on the faces of the mother and daughter who were just below on the bed. The 15 year lad was talking on his mobile when the excessive voltage blasted the internal power reserve of the handset along with his head.

3 days 5 minutes—Everyone pictured was eliminated.

Before any rescue forces could come to the spot, there came a car near the still burning house. The young researcher stepped out of the car and stepped into the ruins carrying in his hand the portable device locator.

"Let me see if it has survived the blast!" Kris said to himself. On the way he saw dead bodies of a girl and a woman near the device location.

"Pretty well!" he exclaimed after looking at them. The camera was well protected below a broken part of the roof which was removed with a bit of effort. Then he picked up the camera and walked laughing over the dead bodies.

Unknown to Kris, however, Sheemal Jezebeth was also observing the device. Breaking the rules at his place; was not that he would let go easily. The next day he called the junior with his camera.

"Keep this device with me for some time." SJ said to him.

For an hour or so, Sheemal just stared at the camera. 'This is one of the most innovative of the devices which have come up in here. Good things must be rewarded with a gift.' SJ thought to himself and called Kris inside. He congratulated the junior and as a token of appreciation, presented him a state of the art personal media player and an appreciation holograph. Kris was surprised with the new found appreciation. Very happy he returned to his work place.

There is a GATE CONTROL theory in medicine which states that if mild pressure is applied near a site of pain, the intensity of the latter is decreased. Similarly, if any of the senses is stimulated above its threshold it will suppress the other senses and activities for the period of the stimulation.

Location—Kris's House.

Kris sat in his house watching a TV programme on his 72 inch LED display. Few minutes later he switches of the display. He then picks up the Media Device presented to him, plugs in the audio canal earplugs and enjoys the virtual 9.2 surround.

The cumulative timer scrolls past minutes. At 00:32:55 the device display turns hazy and goes blank. Kris taps repeatedly on the display. The next second he collapses on the floor as, a high intensity sound tear's through his brain like a hurricane through a thatch house. His eye pupils dilate to maximum, his hands and legs fall loose, and the blood stops in its place. A minute or so later the sound tears his eardrum and 5 seconds later the 3 small bones of his ear disintegrate as blood flows out of his ear. 2 minutes later the blood has started clotting inside his body.

5 Minutes later—Kris is just a mass of solid blood and bones.

The same night a thief breaks into the house and ransacks the house completely and puts all the goods in a goods carrier. He however keeps the Media Device in his hand. At 0400hrs, after the heist he drives into a residential palace and presses the doorbell.

"Your work is done boss!" the thief says on the intercom device outside the door.

Sheemal Jezebeth opens the door. He has his Bluecover Communication Device in his left hand. The thief puts forward the Media Device to him. SJ however refuses to take it.

"Keep it as your reward." He says to the thief in addition to handing him a wad of 1000 rupee notes.

"I don't need it. I can get 1000 times the amount from the loot I got. Thanks to you." The thief tries to be friendly than usual. SJ smiles and pats him on his back. The thief keeps the device beside him in the goods carrier.

Inside his house, SJ opens the 'Triangulation' application on his Bluecover Communication Device and enters the code of the Media Device. The application locates the device and displays its real-time position.

"He is now on the highway." SJ says aloud to himself. He goes to device options and clicks 'ENABLE SATELLITE ASSISTED DETONATION' and sets the timer to 1 minute. He looks at the wall in front of him which has many sticky notes on it. He picks up one blank sticky note, scribbles something on it, sticks it on the wall and retires to sleep. The note reads 'Senior's always have a trick up their sleeve . . .'

At the same time, the thief was in haste to reach the other city to earn riches. With one hand he fiddles with the device whose display suddenly comes alive. Some sequential words appear on the display; which make no sense to the thief.

The display reads,

<DEVICE TRIANGULATION COMPLETE– CONNECTING TO DATABASE–RETRIEVING DEVICE INFORMATION–INITIATING SATELLITE WEAPONRY–SATELLITE WEAPON LAUNCHED–

DELETING DEVICE INFORMATION–DETONATION ACTIVE–OUTSTANDING TIME 15 SECONDS>

The display again turns hazy and then black. Seconds later the thief stops as he sees a bright light approaching his truck from the sky. The missile blasts the goods carrier and its driver to pieces.

Location—Bluecover Corp.

Years later, in January a young doctor shook everyone with her revolutionary finding. Many seniors refuted her findings stating reasons of her age and lack of experience. The visual proof which she displayed finally put a seal on her ability and dedication to work. She was now one of the highest paid employees in BLUECOVER Corp.

6 January

The young and beautiful doc walked down the lobby of her chamber to the conference room. Her face beamed confidence to everyone. Some looked sceptically, some with respect and most with lust. She walked to the speaker's podium, and threw a glance at the empty chairs. A minute later she saw many old scientists pouring in, now the room was packed. She started her speech . . .

"Respected seniors, I would . . . ." She was cut short;

Dr. Pratyush Dhage

"Spare the crap Avnika, get to the point!" A senior shouted.

"OK." DR. Avnika switched of the snazz book and continued, "I procured all the analyses and the tests from our labs and found a simple interesting fact which for all these years had been hidden from all of us!"

"Don't riddle the talk miss . . ." An impatient lady shouted.

"Sure, well I took one sample and carried out a simple specific IOD test and found a substance called as 9232HES."

"Wrong young lady, I've done all the tests myself and this one more than 50 times and never have I encountered any unknown substance in both of the samples." An old doc plunged in between.

"I never said BOTH THE SAMPLES, Did I?" Avnika's voice had a first hint of sarcastic victory.

"What do you mean?"

"All this time these samples were being taken from either of the springs separately. No one cared to hover a few more feet away and take a sample from the confluence of those."

"But when nothings special in both the samples then how can the mixture have a result? Sorry to say but you have been mistaken."

"I'm not, don't you all remember that Acid+Alkali=Salt???" And she made a question mark in the air at all the blank faces.

"Is it a salt then?"

"No it isn't, that was just an analogy to simplify it."

"Then what is it?" came another impatient question.

"I would tell it in one go, if you all don't interrogate me."

She continued, "From the analysis done over each and every sample everyone amazingly missed out on 2 things, one—ESH in the hot spring, two—9323D in the cold spring. These two things combine to form a single THING which I found and called 9232HES in the confluence. Since a small amount of child's brain is always an inseparable part of research, did I chance upon this discovery . . ."

"Don't they separate?"

"They do, but by that time it's something else . . ."

"What do you mean? And how is it related to the tumour?"

"It's not a tumour, and it's this 9232HES thing which is causing this condition." Avnika replied.

"So what is compound exactly?" An old lady said indifferently.

"Well, again, I did not say a COMPOUND, did I?"

"What do you mean?" the impatience had reached its realm.

"It's not a compound; it's a DAMN LIVING THING . . ." DR. Avnika said victoriously.

This declaration made everyone jump in their seats. Everyone forgot the scepticism; each eye was now focussed at the young doc.

"But doctor how does it explain the condition? Is it a virus?" the tone had now changed.

"No it's not a virus; it's more primitive in evolution of the earth, a different line of evolution which got lost somewhere. Viruses require just a host-substrate to be activated. This thing requires the two parts to combine become alive. They combine to produce an orange coloured pulverize which is microscopic. Its mechanism of action is also at the microscopic level."

"Continue doctor, this is Indian history in the making." The first compliment.

"The pulverise, when it comes in contact with the human skin, specifically the palm and sole; rests on the elevation of the skins friction ridge, from the ridge it travels in the maze of depressions of the skin or the finger print to reach the wrist or ankle and from there, it burrows down into the dorsal aspect, and then along the tunica of the artery to the long bone. This bone is the basic requirement of the thing to survive and reproduce."

"How do you know all that?"

"Let's see it live!" and DR. Avnika walked to her LAB with the grand group.

Inside the lab were 2 containers with amputated legs and arms. She led the group to the first set of arm and leg. There they could see the cross section of the organs placed inside formalin. It showed the normal bone and muscle structure.

"These are the normal ones . . . now let's see the affected ones."

DR. Avnika pressed a button. A robotic extension took out an organ from a separate container and placed it in a new dry one.

2 clasps locked it to the base and high speed rotating blades made 4 pieces of the organ at specific levels.

Level 4—At the Elbow
Level 3—Mid Arm
Level 2—Wrist
Level 1—Finger

And similar for the leg.

All the 4 level were put to view by the mechanism, and the container was filled with formalin. A wireless, chemical and acid proof camera inside the container streamed the images to the UHCHD Projector.

Level 4 and Level 3 showed the complete loss of the bone and marrow; Level 2 showed puffed up and defaced arteries and Level 1 magnified view of the finger print region showed excessive deepening of the depressions.

The microscopic view showed the orange pulverise on the ridge elevation. Even the track of descent from the finger print region to the elbow was microscopically marked by the pulverise.

"What happens when the bone is finished??"

"Then it migrates back to the elevations to rejoin the pulverise, then it spreads via touch, it's the most contagious organism ever known to us, even 10 times more than the E and L Virus. Once in the blood stream it can even spread through hair fall as it also has an affinity to the hair follicle."

"And I would like to call it VETOX."

DR. Avnika stopped her explanation. Loud clapping filled the room and she turned pink blushing over that newly gained super respect in the Bluecover Corp Labs. She was promoted the second highest position in her department with a substantial raise.

8 months later Bluecover Corp isolated VETOX. DR. Avnika was given the responsibility of the complete genome mapping of it and she did the job with perfection.

With the complete ssDNA map at the VETOX at their hands the Labs were successful in creating it in artificial culture. The discoverer was promoted to the top most position in her department.

———— ◌∞◌ ————

I was in my clinic winding up for the morning. My cell phone vibrated and its LED flickered violet.

"Heyyyyy Yasssshhhh . . . !" Anvi happily shouted in my ear.

"Hey hey what happened? Very happy you seem to be? Did a filling properly or what???" I teased a joke.

"How mean was that Dr. Yash? Bye . . . !" She faked anger.

"Joking sweetheart!" I giggled. "Now tello what happened . . . ?"

"Avni's got a raise . . . And she's gifted me a biggg performance upgrade on my car, a MUGEN Kit, Pete's box and an ECU remap . . ."

"Your friend is on a remap spree I suppose?" I cracked another joke.

"Ha ha ha . . . so doc we will be coming to your house tonight, be ready." And she disconnected.

The way she said 'BE READY' meant a time for FAST, DARK FUN PACED UP WITH EPINEPHRINE to the maximum.

My cell again vibrated with the violet LED.

"Hmmm . . . . Darling??" I said.

"Forgot to tell ya something . . ." Anvesha said utmost softly.

"What?" I asked softly too.

"Yash, I_____Love _____ You." She said warmly keeping a short silence between the words. It was so intense that I got goose bumps on my complete body.

"Love you too sweetheart, what happened?" I fumbled.

"Love you dear . . . !" she said in the same tone.

"Hey hey now you are raising my BP!" I said with a dry throat.

"Really???? Hee hee." She giggled.

"So I still have the same effect on you after all these years." She chipped.

"Well that's your everlasting love effect sweetie." I pampered her. I think she blushed there coz she said "You naaa . . ." and disconnected the call.

That evening I was thinking about the morning thing while doing the patient. After a few more patients I heard 2 loud horns outside and a minute later 2 knocks on my door.

"Doc you inside?" A soft voice glided inside and someone peeked inside. It was Avnika. "Hey, you both wait in the VIP lounge." I said.

"Okies" She said and the door closed. 15 minutes later I finished the patient and went outside to find them chit chatting.

Both of them had kinds of gothic outfits on and that typical Black eyeliner which gave a kind of sinister tinge to their looks, attitude and personalities.

"So doc, how's your new car doing?" Avnika popped a question as she picked up a model of a tooth.

"My car is . . . ." I struggled to find a perfect word as I looked at them. They presented a menacing look to my eyes.

"Are you feeling afraid of us?" Avni asked.

"No . . . not at all. Er.. um.. yes . . ." I said then thought. They both giggled at first and then burst out laughing.

"Let's go home." I said quietly.

"Your mother won't like us in this avatar." Anvesha said looking at herself.

"You both can relax in the next door flat. Its empty and I sometimes spend free time there." I came out with an acceptable option.

After we came out Anvesha showed me the MUGEN Badge on both the cars, and now the exhaust sound had turned meaty. "Cool, that sound seems speed hungry."

"Don't we?" Anvesha pulled me close and said. "Yes you do . . ." I fumbled and said as Anvi opened the car door for me.

They both went quietly inside the flat and I into my mine and had my dinner made by mum. After watching TV for half an hour I went to the other flat. In the mean time I had got 25 missed calls from Anvi, for time pass.

"So doc should we proceed?" Avnika Asked.

"No no the roads will have some remnant traffic still, we'll go at 1:30AM."

So sitting there we had talks jokes as Anvesha told funny things from her college. Avnika however did not reveal much about her work. I picked up my video camera, tripod and at 1:45AM, we left quietly without waking anyone in the surroundings.

"Where do we go?" Anvesha asked as she opened the door of her car with the key—manually. I had never seen her do that since the day I had met her.

"Somewhere, outside the residential premises of the city, an unused airstrip there." I said as I saw a hint of gleam in their eyes.

"Lead us!" Avnika said as she switched on all the neon's of her vehicle. Within 20 minutes we were there. 8 open lanes of ecstasy. My car was speeding at 125kmph when the girls had been blinking the high beams nearly 50 times a minute.

"Will you race?" Anvi asked innocently.

"Me . . . ? I'll be only halfway in my car by the time you would finish it all." I laughed and said.

"You can have mine if you want to . . . ?" She again said very innocently with a smile. "Ok." I agreed.

Avnika clasped a camera on Anvesha's car's boot and one on her car's bonnet. "We can see the action too . . ." She added.

"Ok then, all set. I'll go to the finish line and signal you both with this green led torch." I picked the large dual focus led torch and said. The girls showed me thumbs up—MEANLY.

"Here, this also . . ." Anvesha said as she removed a conical road marker from her car's boot. It reminded me of a famous open source media player.

"Superb!" I said as I kept that on my car's co-driver seat.

I reached the supposed finish line. It was a 9km stretch. I placed the marker at 8.5km and stood next to it and raised my hands. In reply they both blinked their purple tinged headlights twice. They were impatiently ready . . . I switched on the green led and in a swift movement brought it down . . . "GO . . . !!!!!" I shouted.

For a second I saw the headlights bob up and then down. I quickly took out my video cam. It had a speed calculator too . . . I zoomed up to the cars. They seemed majestic as they gulped the meters in seconds and left clouds of dust behind. Both the cars were nose to nose as they pierced the air at triple digit speeds. I quickly placed my cam on the tripod and focused it at the marker and went close to the road. Both the cars were approaching at a ferocious pace, I stepped back. Both of them zapped past the marker and a cloud of dust engulfed me completely and the marker toppled over. I saw the super LED taillight and a sound of squealing tires as they both pulled the handbrakes. I walked to them, and as I did that, I could smell burnt rubber.

"Hey Yash, I topped at 198kmph!" Anvi was on cloud 9.

"Yessssss . . . . I too did the same albeit 196 at the end . . ." Avnika too was at the same address.

"Who won?" A combined question popped out of the 2 mouths.

"Let us see it!" I said, as I picked up the cam.

"Coooool doc, you made a video of us????" Avnika said in delight.

"Do you mean to say that I am cool or that I made the video is cool?" I popped. Both the girls squinted one eye and gave me a look. "Give that to me." Anvesha snatched the cam from my hands.

We saw the video in slow motion and it was a ravishing one. Anvesha won, thanks to the jutting fenders on her car bumpers.

"Hey that's not fair!" Avnika said pretending fake in a childish tone and we had laugh over it.

Anvesha ran to her car and kissed its windscreen. "My sweetheart, love you lots."

Seconds later she ran up to me and clutched my arms. I saw her nail paint, it was BLACK, but it suited her look. "Now, your turn!" She said to me.

"My car! It not tuned, and anyways I'll lose . . ."

"Spidey spidey, teach my sir a lesson, tell him to have some funnn . . ." she recited a self made poem, looked at the dark sky for 2 seconds, then at me and hushed.

"Ok." I said.

"Yessss!" she said with her mouth and hands and gave me a tight hug. With her gothic looks I could not call her hug a cute one!

"Here . . . !" she said handing me the keys of her car, and took mine.

"I'll place the marker midway on the track. You both will come from opposite sides. Whoever reaches first . . . . got it??????" Anvi said ending with a question mark.

"Yes babe!" we both contestants said. Anvesha looked at me with a vicious smile, winked at both of us.

"Ok then Avnika, reach that point, and Yash you to the other end." Our leader added.

"Yup." We agreed as she sat in my car.

"And when I bring the light down, you start." She engaged 4*4 in my car, wheel spinned all the tires, created a large cloud of smoke and raced off. I took to my track. I always had problem spinning wheels so I avoided smoking her car tires.

Anvesha had now setup the tripod. She held the led torch high, Avnika blinked her car halogens and so did I. she let the green led's down. Avnika's car lights went up and then down.

I pressed the throttle halfway down and let go off the clutch. The car surged forward with an awesome force which pressed my complete spine harder on to the backrest. The force this time was much greater that the last time I had driven this car. The tuning thing had worked wonders with the beauty of my beauty. I sucked the maximum juice by reaching the maximum possible speed limit of each gear. The engine made a throaty roar as car surroundings turned into a blur and the RPM needle played a race between the digits 7 and 8.

2nd at 40, 3rd at 80, 4th at 125, 5th at 170 and finally the 6th at 190kmph—all within 30seconds. Her car had an astonishing love for speed. I looked at the speedometer needle; it was still away from the maximum speed number. I saw as it counted the numbers. The marker was coming close and the raucous howl of the engine told that it was not full yet and still hungry for more throttle, so I pressed the pedal to the floor. The exhaust roared fire as the car accelerated to 195kmph when Avnika zapped passed me and I crossed the marker. The drag ended, an adrenaline pumping fun which lasted 55 seconds. I pressed the brakes and turned the car back as I saw a cloud of dust in front of me.

"Hey Anvesha . . . I did a 195kmph!" I shouted to her.

"But, Avni won . . ." Anvesha halted twice while saying this. "But you had won na cutie . . ." I said to her.

Avnika came very happy, "Hey I did 198 this time . . ."

"And you won too . . ." We both said cheerfully. "Yipeeeeeee . . ." Avnika shouted like a kiddie who had won a Barbie doll in a lucky draw.

We saw the video. I was a cool 2 feet away from the marker when Avnika had zapped past at a relative speed of 393kmph. Avnika unstrapped the camera from the boot. "I'm going to watch this in my relaxing room." She said as she showed us the videos. The noise making wheel spin looked fantastic, the approaching of 195 was over the top, and finally "In the face at 393kmph" was breathtakingly awesome. By the time we finished it was nearly 4:30.

Avnika wanted to go but Anvesha did not allow her and made off with her car giving her the keys of my GYPSY leaving me to drive her car . . . confused???? I was driving Anvesha's car, Anvesha was driving Avnika's and Avnika was driving mine.

We reached home at 5:15AM; some people were out for morning walks. They both went into the flat and slept and I went inside mine.

At around 11AM I was in my clinic when a soft voice glided inside and someone peeked inside. "Doc, you inside?" Avnika said.

"Hi, good morning . . ." I replied.

"Ya ya, we just came to say bye . . . it was fun." She said. "It sure was." I added.

"One more thing?"

"Yes?"

"Can I take this tooth model?" Avnika picked up the life size model of the tooth she was holding last night.

"Yes . . ." I said casually. "It's kind of cute . . ." she said and left.

Location—BLUECOVER Corp.

The purpose with which the labs were built in India was now fulfilled. The isolated organism was photographed with The Titan 80-300 Cubed microscope and along with the name of the discoverer placed in the HALL OF SUCESS of BLUECOVER.

DR. Avnika felt proud when she saw her name in platinum letters at the top of the list.

Within a few weeks the labs reared the deadly organism in artificial culture media. India was now ready with one of the most deadly and horrifying weapon of biological warfare. The way the organism killed a human was one of the most pitiable and brutal death he could die. Arms legs were reduced to rolls of flesh hanging from the body with minor ossification. It was also one of the most painful deaths because the pain was not suppressed even by general anaesthesia when the organism reached the marrow portion. The organism just devoured the bone and blood as we would chomp on a pizza.

In October, giving a finger to the peace treaties around the world, Indian Defence announced their entry into the world's deadliest biological weapon arsenal and released the pictures of the mangled dead bodies to the world especially to the USA, Pakistan and China.

US came in the news stating that they would find and destroy the arsenal.

"A new terrorist comes and craps on your face every month with a new tape and you bastards now want to mess with us. We'll show you what we are now!" Sheemal Jezebeth said on the TV.

A few days later on BBC-

"Bloody, they do research with our people in Chicago and try to be an ace with us . . . I'm going to show them who's the BIG MOUTH and who's the BOSS now!"

"What do you plan to do?" the interviewer asked, a bit afraid.

"Something; which the world has never seen before!" Sheemal Jezebeth sneered.

The atmosphere in the Labs was electrified. They had got a very large grant from the Indian govt via the defence wings. The defence was now freely funding what it thought was a waste of money since AD 2000. rDNA technology was used to create 26 grade mutations in the organism which became so virulent that it could reach the bone in 3 minutes and even cross 7 latex glove protection. A strain independent of the path of entry was created. This was so powerful that it killed a person due to lung liquefaction in 2 minutes. Also they made it such that it would only infect not spread.

In 2006 the labs had created a weapon which could decompose neurons. However it took 15days to take action and caused motor loss with 70% sensory loss. It wasn't practical as an instant biological weapon. Efforts were on to increase the virulence and combine it with the newest weapon. 6 weeks later, efforts met success and an independent strain with bone and neuron munching capability was created.

The Labs were doing tests on the unclaimed bodies found in hospitals, medical colleges, railway stations, morgues. Bodies unclaimed for 7 days were being sent to labs. And with a population of millions there was no scarcity of them . . .

The strain created a blob of the skull and brain in 3 minutes. The mass of flesh, eyes and hair lying in a pool of blood made such a gore picture that many of the researchers turned neurotic in the lab premises due to the extreme brutality. India was on its way to become the most deadly stock of biological brutality in the world.

However the Indian Defence had something else in mind. They were not satisfied with the experiments carried out on dead creatures. They wanted to see it work on ENEMIES!

Days later, the news were riot with news of another militancy surge in J&K specifically POK. The defence had enough of those bastards for the past decades. Without giving a second thought, orders were given to the army to retreat from the region. The process was carried at an emergency scale and told in the news. Within a week infiltration increased 10 times. Now was the perfect time for Sheemal Jezebeth's quote to come true.

45 planes with android pilots were sent and the created organism was sprayed over the complete region like DDT of the Stone Age.

This operation was named as WIPE-OUT . . . and what it met with was called in the Indian media as Brutal Success. Within 2 hours the complete area was devoid of anything that could move by its own wish. Another plane was sent to bring the state of success achieved. The data that the plane brought was supposed to be censored before release according to the rules of broadcasting, but it was not.

Guns, bombs, clothes, chains, shoes, eyeballs, hair, fingernails, hooves, horns, fur, teeth, exposed portions of the abdomen, vital organs lying in litres of mucous, blood and in the snow made the bloodiest picture ever seen by humans worldwide.

During the last week of October a study carried out ranked the IAF as the 2nd best, INS as the 3rd best and the Indian Army as the Best in the world. News channels were chock-a-bloc with the latest news. The gory picture of POK had played havoc with the world peace.

Worldwide research had begun on creating the most horrible and deadly Biological Weaponry. Success met was being freely advertised and exposed. Norway came out with a chemical which could freeze blood to -18 degrees Celsius in flat 5 minutes so that when the bodies fell to the ground they broke to pieces. Sweden was up with an invention which could straighten out the *villi* of the stomach and intestines so that the stomach felt full without eating anything and the body digested itself.

Germany was back to Nazism, they brought to life which was called as the 'ANHILATOR'—It drained or rather osmosed the fluid contents of the body as sweat in half an hour and what remained resembled the mummies of Egypt.

Egypt was never in the race of all these things but the weapon which they brought to light was one of the weirdest one. It was made from a compound procured from the meteor-strike site in Central Sahara. It dried up the body's joint fluid in flat

10 minutes. It converted the body into a machine without lubrication such that the people died due to excruciating pain on trying to move even their fingers.

A new kind of a race was on in the world. Governments legalized the use of these weapons on militants, Maoists, underworld encounters, drug lords, drug-traffickers, child abusers, sexual abusers and body traffickers. Samples were being sent in jailhouses to test them on the most hardcore of the criminals. In Islamic countries these were brought as gold to be used in for the punishment of sex crimes. Human right activists were on each and every road in all countries including India to persuade people to help them stop the use of these, but none supported them because it was the first time in the human evolution that insurgent attacks, militant terror, illegal trafficking, sex rackets and sex related crimes had come down by 95% worldwide. The images which were released were gore enough to cause heart failures in 80% of the general population. Criminals were being awarded final punishments in front of other inmates to scare the shit out of them. And this strategy was working without any resistance worldwide. Biology of the Dark Side had gotten a gore grip over minds worldwide; it had broken the Courage in every unfeeling and\or fearless person present on the earth crust.

The opposite forces did a lot to obtain the arsenal with a lot cash and kind but met with no success.

The defence officials worldwide, knew that if they fell in trap there was no road back. Those things could proverbially seal the world's fate.

— ∞∞∞ —

On that day watching TV, I was thrilled to know that the Indian Forces were the supreme in the world. This was the topic of discussion in the newspapers now. I felt even more proud to be citizen of the new superpower INDIA. In a poll conducted by many newspapers and channels, the public came out with a staggering 98% YES to the use of those weapons on militants and in terror matters. Never before in my life had I seen the public give such a strong opinion on any matter till now. I suppose it was because our so called friend Pakistan was involved . . . ha ha ha . . . A few of my patients also came over and talked about those things.

On a Sunday after finishing early we both were at a sip-spot sitting opposite of each other. Anvesha had a black Tee on, with sky blue jeans, tied up hair as a pony tail. She looked cute . . . no no . . . very very cute. We had ordered orange juice. The juice looked enticing as it touched her pink lips. She looked like a dream always, no wonder I loved looking at her and wanted to do that for the rest of my life.

She lifted her hand and took it to the clutcher in her hair and opened it slight. A few of her hair came to play on her face in a flash second.

"Hey what are you doing?" that surprised her.

"What did I do?" she asked looking at herself and around. Her hand was still on her clutcher which was half open.

"Don't let your hair open!" I chipped.

"Why so?" she asked cutely as she bent her neck to the right. Err . . . her right.

"I'll not be able to speak." I said.

"Eh???" she said with a question mark on her face.

"You look enticingly beautiful with your hair open; I don't find words to say when you are like this." I stopped and she let the clutcher off her hair. All the strands were now free to fall on her neck, face and cheeks. Her pink lips and pearly whites looked exhilaratingly beautiful as they peeped from those jet black hair as she giggled over my so called cute appreciation. When she laughed even her eyes smiled and they were oceans of innocence and love for me.

I rested my cheek on my palm and looked at her.

"Say something . . ." she said.

Dr. Pratyush Dhage

"You know?" I asked.

"What should I know?" she asked back.

"That you are so beautiful." I said lost in her eyes.

"Yes sure . . ." and she ruffled my hair and pulled my nose.

"Let's go for a stroll . . ." she said as she quickly paid for the juice.

"It was my turn to pay." I protested which only drew a toothy smile from her.

"Where shall we go?" I asked her.

"Ummm, to a temple, long time since I went to one." She said and we walked to nearby temple.

In the temple we said a short prayer in our minds. When I opened my eyes she still had her eyes closed. A glimpse of how she might look while taking a nap.

She took out a box from her pocket. From it she took out a gold ring and slid it on to my left hand ring finger. I tried to say something but she put her finger on my lips and walked out.

"Now you are locked to my network." She in her techno talk announced that we both were now made for each other.

We took her car to a scenic location, with a water reservoir at one side and a range of mountains at the other.

"I love you." I said squeezing her hand. In return she gave me a light hug and rested her head on my shoulder. We sat there till the sun went down and after that. By the time we reached home it was 0930hrs, too dark and the traffic was just indescribable, so I insisted that she spend the night at our next door flat which was generally empty. She called her mom to ask that.

"Mom, can I stay at his house. I'm dead tired and too much traffic." She said on the phone.

"Moooooommmm! Yes." Anvesha's face turned red as her mom replied something.

"Ok mom, bye! Yyyyyes mom sure!" her face turned redder as she disconnected. Seconds later she slyly looked at me.

"Hey what happened?" I asked. She kept quiet. I asked again, but she was still quiet. I poked her more.

"Actually my mom wanted to confirm if your parents were at home or not!" Anvesha turned into a ripe strawberry and I burst out laughing like a lunatic complete for 5 minutes.

"Shut up! You don't have a sister, you will never understand it." she said, still a strawberry.

"Heh heh . . . I understand." And once again I burst out laughing. This time; like an idiot. I just could not stop.

She went in to the other flat. After an hour she called me. She squatted on the bed and I sat on the chair. She looked immensely cute squatting like that. We talked a lot that night for about 3 hours. When she felt sleepy, she lied down. I looked at her, her hair came down on her face. I moved my hand on her face and adjusted her hair.

"You know, I have received a boon from god!" I said.

"What?" she asked quietly.

"You, my Anvesha!" I said and she gave her best smile. After a few minutes she fell asleep. I looked at her sleeping for over half an hour. She looked like a fairytale with her eyes closed. I turned down the temperature of the AC and went to the exit door but remembered something and turned back. I pulled the comforter over her and she tugged it in sleep. I bended and gave a soft kiss on her forehead and left the flat.

EUPHRATES RIVERSIDE RESEARCH CENTRE

A group of historians and archaeologists had been working for the past many years on the importance of the Euphrates River in history. Although the importance of it has already been emphasized in the various scriptures, this time the historians were up to something new.

There has been a mention in scriptures of something as the largest treasure in the world, and the secret of it is hidden in the Euphrates. The group had been working over the river for a period of 10years.

Over the time lapse, the place had provided them a lot of information of and about the evolution of the humans, religion, the education of mankind on peace and self recognition and finally the ultimate aim of life the Divine Moksha. There was one tablet unearthed which told the crux of life on how it should be lead in 13 points. It stated the following;

1. If you want to drink—Drink your Anger.
2. If you want to forget—Forget your Sorrows.
3. If you want to swallow—Swallow your Disrespect.
4. If you want to give—Give Alms.
5. If you want to gain—Gain Knowledge.
6. If you want to win—Win Love.
7. If you want to show—Show Kindness.
8. If you want to lose—Lose your Pride.
9. If you want to hear—Hear the appreciation of others.
10. If you want to ask—Ask for spiritual satisfaction.
11. If you want to speak—Speak the truth.
12. If you want to throw—Throw Jealousy out.
13. If you want to do—Go Serve the Poor.

This tablet was the centre piece of attraction at the centre as many left the maddening hunt for the elusive treasure. However it was soon destroyed because this is the age of material happiness, so even though the various other tablets which were unearthed from the river over the years were a treasure of information, there was a mad hunt for wealth which was mentioned in holy texts . . .

"A wealth of unbound abundance, a tease of a hyper human latitude, an amount so large that would make every person on the earth a king of his dreams, a treasure so huge that it would not fit even in the eyes of the people who would see it, the sparkle of which would stun every eye which would see it and a trove of such an astounding proportion which would satisfy every GREED on the planet."

Over the years the historians were working under the guise of educational purposes but the real reason was clear. During the initial years of research there was a daily analysis of the reports by agencies of the country government experts. However when they saw that the real purpose was not being fulfilled, the interest weaned and gradually the place lost attention. Bluecover corp however did not feel the same way. They sent a one of their junior researcher as an intern to the group to convey the daily progress. This was 5 years ago. Years passed everyday only the same news would come . . .

One day . . .

"Hey, help me get this out will yaa . . . I've bumped on ta sumthin . . ." An American archaeologist shouted as his foot struck something hard in the river bed.

One of his colleagues sent a few workers to pick whatever it was. They all came and groped for the thing. After a few unsuccessful attempts, they found the hard thing. All tried to pull it out and after a minute of force it came unstuck from the sand. It was something which resembled a small treasure chest. It was just 1100hrs but the work for the day was stopped and then all those who worked assembled in the discussion room to see the so called treasure chest. There ensued a lengthy discussion which went on for 13-20hours. Over the time many scientists came examined the chest and tried to decipher the script and open the box but could not. On detailed examination it was found that it was not a single thing but a conglomeration of various devices.

The chest was an ancient thing. It had 5 layers.

That night after the researchers and scientists left for their tents, the intern entered the tent in which the chest was kept. He took out a device from his pocket and placed it on the hinges of the enclosure in which the chest was placed and switched it on. 5 minutes later the hinges had melted away. He picked up the lid from the box and placed the chest on the floor and looked at it. After a thorough thinking of over what he thought the mechanism might be he pressed an embedded gem on the lid of the chest.

As he pressed the gem a tray slid out making a sound. He took off the cover on the tray. Beneath it was a plethora of assorted gold coins. His eyes sparkled as he saw them. Between the sparkly mass was a big one, the size of a small lid, black in colour and the shiniest of the lot. He tried to pick it up but it did not move, as a reflex he pushed it. There was the same sound and one more tray slid out. This one was filled with coins which were of silver and in the same way were 2 black coins in the center of the drawer. With 2 fingers he pressed those 2 and after the same sound a third level came out. This one was filed with coins of bronze and 3 black coins in the center. In the next level were iron coins with 5 rusted black coins. Each time the black coins increased and the amount of the valuable treasure decreased, and the last he opened was not valuable. He looked at the chest in sheer amazement. Why had the others not been able to see which he was able to do in a few moments? Then he realized that, "This cannot be the treasure, this is too small, and its maximum valuation will reach approximately 200 crores." He tried to pick up the chest to see it, but now it did not budge from the floor.

He crawled around the chest and found some inscription near the base of the chest. He translated it,

'The cycle of the ages will tell humans a message. A hope lies in for the world, only if it knows how to read it.'

"What does it all mean?" he said to himself.

He looked more diligently around the chest to find any more hints but couldn't.

He opened the first drawer and picked up the gold coins and emptied the drawer and just stared at the black coin. Surprisingly he could now pick up the black coin. He realized that all those were on a piece of parchment. He took it out. There were some words written on it.

'Purity and love is the way for humans. A time before time when material bliss was all but absent, life was as white as diamonds and pure as gold.'

He opened the 2nd drawer and took out the second parchment.

'With the passage of time, the human kind will encounter evil in the most unexpected way. The vice can be left behind and shall be left behind.'

Next, without thinking he pulled out the 3rd parchment.

'Mankind is devoid of thought, and haste will occur. The stone will now be seen as the savior.'

Then, the 4th one.

'Evil will come from all sides, good will have a different face, the face will be black. Greed is the limit. Vice will be the field, hatred will be sowed and malice will be reaped.'

As soon as he read the parchment it crumbled and disintegrated to ash. The 5 rusted coins rose up inside. And so also did 5 gems rise on the lid of the chest and glowed. He pressed the rusted coins, but nothing happened. He tried it twice but nothing changed. Then, after a thought he kept the fingers of his other hand on the 5 glowing gems and pressed the rusted black coins and as he did that, the other 4 levels made a sound and closed shut. The gold silver and bronze coins were reduced to ash and the 5th level made a just a click sound.

The intern looked at the events in astonishment but now he feared the ambience and happenings . . . he pulled open the 5th level. A black smoke came out from the chest and filled the tent with a stench which resembled a mortuary and reduced the visibility inside the tent to zero.

He ran out of the tent to avoid suffocation. No one was awake in there. After the smoke cleared half an hour later, he went inside again. The chest was as before only the 5th drawer was out. There was a parchment in it. He looked at the parchment. It was blank. Below it was a cover. He took the cover off and as he looked inside his face went pale. It was filled with degraded bones dipped in fresh blood. He shrank away from the chest in terror. Euphrates was not what he expected.

It was all over his mind now. He ran away with the parchment to his tent. He was so scared that holding the parchment steadily was out of the question for the next half hour. He looked at his Bluecover Communication device. The info light was continuously blinking.

"Oh god, sir was calling for the daily report, gotta give him the news . . ."

He called in the office but the call was transferred to Sheemal Jezebeth's device. At home Sheemal was waiting for the report.

"Yes, where were you? How dare you break the protocol?"

"Sorry sir but much has happened today that I've just finished getting away from it." The intern blurted out in a single breath.

"What????? Describe it in detail." SJ ordered. The intern gave all the details and stopped at the blank parchment.

Dr. Pratyush Dhage

"Blank parchment you say, it can't be blank there might be a hidden message or location of the treasure on it. Teleport it to me. You'll get it back in an hour." The intern kept it in the teleporter, and pressed the TRANSFER button.

"Ok, I've received it." SJ said and disconnected the talk device.

Shemal Jezebeth held the parchment in his hand. Then he examined it with his magnifying roller device. One and a half hours later he had a face which radiated happiness. He kept the parchment back in the teleporter and then messaged him, 'You have done a great job. You will be one of the 25.'

The intern was surprised. What special had he done by sending a blank paper so as to get a place in the top league?

He opened the latch and took out the parchment. To his amazement it was not blank anymore. He started to read the entire thing;

'The transitional age of the demon has arrived when the degree 5 opens. Humankind does not change and a demonic force takes it into an age of horror. Material bliss is the only satisfaction. In the search of material will the demon unearth the huge treasure of the gods, a treasure of the almighty which can never be touched by the man. For the persuasion of the wealth will the demon

will go to destroy pure white affection with alongside flowing water. When the earth is full of holding hypocrisy, will it take inside the human to reduce the evil at three places, a time comes when the almighty will shun the human and when the human will find solace and safety at their homes rather than with god . . . When this occurs, will the Treasure of Gods be ready to come.

With the treasure in the reach of the demon, the macrocosm will undergo a change, good will occur, but for more evil.

This being the age of the demon, this script can only be read by the demon himself before anyone else can . . .'

The intern fell to the ground. He was devastated when read the last line. Scared, terrified, surrounded by horror, he picked up the gun in his bag and shot himself dead. The demon had been identified but the identity remained a secret from the cosmos. For the rest of the world the demon had died.

⊷⊷⊷

Far away in the forests of Tripura and Nagaland

They were the unexplored forests of the world. No one knew what secret they held. Over the years, the terrain and the unexplainable, unpredictable weather made the total exploration impossible. Even though many ones went deeper inside, nearly all of them returned mysteriously citing loss of interest and more amazingly no one regretted the abandonment of the expedition. All they citied, was that, as they explored more of the woods they felt less enthusiastic of the task and finally decided to abandon it. No one knew the reason, but Time Immemorial did know it and it dated thousands of years back to a curse.

400 kilometers inside the deep of the deepest jungle was a place which was no less than hell. The place, strewn with corpses; the stench, so overwhelming; that all the trees and plants of the place had dried and withered thousands of years ago. Whichever animal entered the region dropped dead. Even vultures, bats, and owls did not come there. Whichever bird flew over the region, dropped dead instantly. The place had been a land of rotting flesh since ages. There were billions of maggots eating out the dead flesh. Bones lay in millions on the ground; every skull had thousands of insects crawling in it. These were the only things which lived in that region of descretion and inhuman insult.

But there was one more being which had survived the horror of the planet over the past ages. A being who wanted death every moment, a being who was sole carrier of all the sins of the world, a being who could never be touched by any disease was the one who had all those which plagued the earth before time could be written, a being who begged for death but whom even the most dreaded and deadliest diseases could not kill.

No beast ventured near the being, even insects shrunk away in horror when the being stepped close. It was the pity of the ages and the neglect of time. It seemed that time as it went by, just forgot about the being, as if time just saw the being lying on the earth between those millions of rotting corpses, and forgot. Wherever the being wandered, it brought misery and loss of hope. Whosoever had seen it past the ages dared not see it again . . . The being was a night mare even for the devil.

It was enormous in proportion, over 12 feet in height and 3-4 feet in width. Over the ages its gait had change from running away to crawling to dragging his ghoul remains.

The skin had turned black and it was full of sores and gaping ulcers bleeding black blood which flowed like a thick paste as it moved. The soles of the palm and feet had given way to bone which made the being writhe in pain as it dragged itself in between the filth. The nails had turned brown-grey in color and had been torn off; instead they curled up from the site of origin. The hands and legs were exposed to the sun as the rotting skin decayed as it hung partially from the body causing a stench which no living organism could stand. The shreds of rubber like skin fell in pieces as it moved. The exposed bones were broken at many places and made a grating noise, but miraculously stayed together. Blood dripped from its bones even as it lied down. Its thigh and abdomen had huge pock marks and rivulets of abscess ran criss-crossing the skin and bones. The skin near the marks peeled off in layers like an onion, as the sky above looked in pity. The abdomen was completely ripped off and internals gaped out to the filth with the blood oozing out. His chest was half bulged out and back was stripped off all the muscles and skin with an enormous hunch. His head had tufts of hair; wherever they grew it was a mesh of blood, pus, dirt, and filth. A part of the lower jaw was broken and the denuded piece of the bone hung from the throat with a group of muscles. The skin of its face had broken off exposing the skull; his bleeding, reticulated, and dry eyes had no eyelids.

The top of his head had a gaping hole in it which exposed the denuded brain throbbing inside the cranial cavity.

The being pulled a piece of rotten flesh from a corpse and thrust it down into its food pipe. Then in a guttural sound he growled . . .

"Why did you curse me with such a life? Why is this dreadful existence a repentance of a mistake I did thousands of years ago? Please give me death, I beg. Release me, release Ashwatthama from this curse. Give me death, give me death, I alone cannot carry the sins of this world now, give me death lord, release me . . ." He howled, the howl made trees go pale and the ground dry. And Ashwatthama collapsed in the filth. His dry eyes teared, and in that filth, they were the only pure things; the pure tears of repentance and of regret. Ashwatthama had been crying for thousands of years and waiting for his release . . .

I was a happy person. There was little wrong in my life. My clinic was running fine and along with a beautiful girl with me I was a happy person. I was very fond of watching and reading mythology. Many of my rather so called friends did not have any knowledge and info about it and were like a dumb child on questions related to mythology. They even said to me-

"Scriptures are just a myth; there is not truth in them . . ." I was disgusted on listening to such things so I stopped talking to all of them.

Sitting in my free time I would read or study about these predictions and stories. They fascinated me. I saw a show which was shown on the TV about religious mythology. They were showing a ritual of hitting stones. Well this fact might not generate interest but there was another thought provoking fact.

Apply logic; when you hit stones at a specific site, they will hit the thing and fall down as a pile. If

it's a hole or so, it will fill up within a short time period. Ok that's it.

The channel showed that the place where the stones fell. There were no stones visible in the enormous pit shown. The caretaker was called upon and interviewed to provide more info.

"Since time immemorial people have been hitting stones at these places and the miracle is that this place never fills up. We've never seen stones piling up in here. Over the past 1000 years people come here by the millions and stones have been hit in billions but no one knows where they disappear. God is great."

Fascinating fact isn't it? But god always has a different plan for all and then came the news which said,

'FOR CENTURIES, PEOPLE HAVE BEEN HITTING THE SATAN. EVEN THE WICKED HAVE DONE IT, AND TODAY THE SATAN HAS HAD ENOUGH BECAUSE THE STONES HITTING HIM WHICH WERE GOING NOWHERE ARE POURING OUT OF THE EARTH.'

⸗∞⸗

Was this a normal phenomenon or was there something else behind all this was a hot topic of guesswork, but it buried fear, a centimetre into the subconscious mind of everyone, was it going to be the most remarkable year of my life? I shuddered to think. All the TV was riot with thoughts of biological warfare and a sure World War.

It was only few days since my darling had put the ring around my finger. I felt so nice to have such a lovely wife to be. With all those thoughts playing in mind, I went to sleep. At around 3 in the night, hundreds of screams woke me up; our building was shaking like anything. It was an earthquake. Everyone was outside the next minute. I took out my mobile and connected it to the live TV on the phone network. It took a while but latched on.

It showed that there had been 3 hyper massive landslides and earthquakes which were measuring over 10 on the Richter scale. I tried to get a satellite snap of the region but due to the quake, everything had slowed down. 2 of those quakes were in totally unexpected regions. The first one was in New York. Approximate casualty was 20 million. The second one was in Saudi Arabia whose epicentere was at Mecca. The third was in an expected location—Tokyo, Japan. Casualty was approximately 25 Million.

1 hour later the satellite link stabilized. I quickly scrolled to NY. It was no longer there; in place of it was a hole 60km wide. U.S was devastated by the quake. Then I scrolled to Japan. I could not see anything special. Then I looked at the symbol showing the epicentre. The quake had ripped past

the country, now the Pacific Ocean divided Japan into two parts. I tried scrolling to Saudi, but the satellite fix went haywire again. By this time the earth shaking had stopped. There was much damage around the world. Our building was one of the earthquake resistant constructions which had developed mild cracks. There was no other option but to go back inside and we did the same.

I lied down on the bed and looked at the crack on the roof. "What if the roof gives away . . . ?" I shuddered to ask myself and in fear, fell asleep. When I woke up, as was expected cable TV was out of order. I again hooked up my cell to the satellite and the thing I saw could beat a science fiction film by a huuuuge margin.

The symbol showing the epicentre was exactly on The Kaaba. A stretch around The Kaaba of around 2km was fine and I could see a lot of faces shouting for help on the live satellite feed. No one was happy or thankful over being in the vicinity of a holy place. After that spot was a circle of crust sinking of diameter 60km starting from The Kaaba, the base of the landslide affected area could not be seen. In the satellite feed it looked like a supersized bull's-eye.

Later that day around 6 hours later, the cable TV networks resumed. The live fed was amazing as defence choppers air lifted people stranded at various parts of the world. After an hour of evacuations another landslide report came in from

Mecca. Now The Kaaba was on a land of diameter of 0.5km.

Location—BLUECOVER Corp.

The 3 massive quakes had done their part of damage to the Labs in India. However with the kind of finances BLUECOVER had, the damages were done well in a matter of a week.

10 days later—Cybernetic Division.

A high profile meeting was in progress. The corporation was now in the search of the mythological treasure of the Taj Mahal. They sent a camouflaged IAF plane in the restricted Taj airspace for an aerial survey of the location. With the tech at BLUECOVER it was a child's play to escape the Stone Age radars.

The special IAF-BLUECOVER Corp plane was loaded with a radiation scanner, hollow out scanner, layer differentiation device, geometric density calculator and a weakest point assessment device. The plane went and came back undetected. It now had a plethora of information related to the Taj Mahal, unknown for years.

A new meeting was held to decide to break the monument to retrieve the treasure.

"Sir, people will wreak havoc over the planet if we even attempt to do anything like that and anyways the hollow-out scans tell that it is just stone on a base of stone and nothing else."

"What the hell are you talking about? Didn't you notice the state of the people when they were stranded near The Kaaba? No one even looked at it! Any ways I'm not concerned with all that."

"But sir it would be against humanity to do such a thing . . ."

"Oh stop that crap . . . !! Do you know the worth of the treasure . . . ??? It's 100,000 times the total wealth on the planet. Do you get it?"

"But our scans can't lie, there's nothing inside it." The junior protested.

"Shut up and reply what you are asked. What does the weakest point assessment say?"

"The weakest point is at the top of the monument dome exactly at the point where the vertical line from the supposed architectural defect is present."

"Defect??"

"The supposed place, from which Shajahan's tears fall on the fake graves."

"What do you mean by 'supposed'?"

"That's because the hollow out scanners tell a different story of the building."

"What do you mean?"

"The base of the Taj Mahal is of the height of 55 meters, and which is basically a group of rooms. Below it is the foundation of the building. It is not built on a completely flat plain. There is a slight elevation in the centre and it is the only portion which is making contact with the complete base."

"That's physically and mechanically impossible. How can such an enormous structure rest and be balanced on a just a small elevation?"

"Sir it seems as such on the scan image, after we apply the edge enhancement, it becomes clear that the complete base is balanced on a very big reservoir of super compressed air because the blank space which we see is closed from all sides."

"Continue the story; it is more than amazing . . ."

"Next, the tear thing, the water which falls from above is not tears but they are a part of the locating mechanism which tells us where exactly the base is in contact with the elevation. The place where a water drop would fall ONLY UNDER THE FORCE OF GRAVITY is the point where the elevation is . . . And if we need to retrieve the supposed treasure we need to strike the elevation with full force."

"What would be the weight required to break it . . . ?"

"If dropped diagonally, or at any other point other than the weakest point, then more than 1000tonnes."

"And?" SHEEMAL JEZEBETH cut him short in eagerness.

"If we drop it vertically on the weakest point then only 100 tonnes from a height of 1024meters." The junior said.

"Sir we will need a 4 stage detonation device before we impact the elevation, specifically a device which will explode at 4 places to make way for the final assail device. First the roof, second the fake grave, third the so called real graves and finally at the foundation."

"Ok is that all?"

"Sir once the foundation is broken, the compressed air shall come out at a very high velocity; it however should not create any problem for us"

"Ok then, The Treasure of Taj Mahal shall soon be ours . . ." SHEEMAL JEZEBETH said and left the cybernetic meeting hall. This was the world's biggest and most dangerous treasure hunt ever to be put in action and hence BLUECOVER Corp pulled up its sleeve.

15 days later.

The BLUECOVER Corp was ready with a 200tonne block of Lead which had a blunt tip of pure Titanium. The tip was cyberneticaly engineered to split the elevation into **4 pieces**.

At 0000hrs, SHEEMAL JEZEBETH ordered the 4 stage detonator and the 200 tonne airlift to take off. The plan was simple, first of all the 200tonne airlift would take off and take to the calculated altitude; next, 8 force field forming choppers would take their places around the Taj Mahal in all the 8 directions to prevent any intrusions or ward off any interference, OF ANY KIND—Vital or Non-Vital . . .

The 8 choppers were fully fledged hyper war devices which could detect and destroy any threat within a range of 600kms. They were specially equipped for automatic weapon launch. The choppers reached the location at 0200hrs and positioned themselves.

Location—The prohibited airspace over The Taj Mahal.

The airlift positioned itself over the Taj Mahal by 0230hrs and was unmanned. It focused green lasers corresponding to the upper 4 corners of the monument and a red laser at the impact point.

———⌘———

I was sleeping rather nicely, when all the commotion outside woke me up.

"Shit, one more earthquake . . ." I said to myself as I saw the crack on the ceiling, again . . .

I rushed out and all I could hear was—people shouting like lunatics. The sound was coming from the streets. I rushed to the main road. Hordes of people were running rummaging public property, burning whatever that could be burnt, shouting slogans against no one in particular. I saw 4 buses, 13 cars, 47 motorcycles, 35 humans burning on the road. It was a devastating site around which I saw in horror. Gore was all alive in front of my eyes. Riots are the worst thing that can occur in any city . . . Some rushed at me with flaming bottles, but I was quicker and was safe inside my house in 2 minutes after a bottle fell 6 feet away from me. A narrow escape it was.

Panting, I switched on the TV to see what had happened, and the thing I saw was the most outrageous psyche out I had ever seen in 29 years of my existence on the planet. I did not know whether I was dreaming or was it the truth; whatever it was . . . God knows, but it was live from Agra.

8 super war ready choppers were surrounding The Taj Mahal. Then they showed another one high up in the air, directly over The Taj Mahal throwing green lasers on it.

All of these were stationery. Channels themselves had sent helicopters to cover the extraordinary sabotage.

Suddenly the screen went blank. I switched the channel. The other channel showed that one of the choppers had bombed one of the media helicopters, coz it went too near.

"So that's why the screen went blank???" I thought.

They showed the high up chopper once again. 2 massive cylinders were hanging from it. I could not guess why it was so . . .

Minutes later the choppers fired a few missiles. 2 minutes later, news flashed that a total of 7 combat planes had been brought down at an approx 400 km from Agra. Out of those, 2 were of the US Army.

I was now sure that some ace person was behind all this. The scale of whatever that was going on was beyond imagination . . . My eyes were glued to the screen. At 2:45AM few seconds later the windshield of the choppers showed a message,

10 SECONDS TO STRIKE.

"What are they going to strike now?" I asked myself.

The countdown started . . . 10, 9, 8, 7, 6, 5, 4, 3, 2, 1 . . . . STRIKE—

The high up chopper let go of the first cylinder, a second later the second one and the former struck right at the centre of The Taj Mahal dome and shattered it with a deafening blast, and the second cylinder followed it inside without sound as a kid would follow a mother.

Seconds later came the scene of another blast inside the Taj as the second one blasted the fake graves. The complete monument was shaking and there was a tornado of emotions in my heart as I remembered visiting the monument and playing inside and around it, and this night the same monument was being razed for I don't know what.

There was another blast, this time it were the real graves, and along with the blast the complete basement of the Taj shattered, the red blocks were dislodged from the holdings as the foundation of monument started to collapse under its weight. The rubble was falling continuously and defacement of the building was reaching its culmination. I could not hold my tears as I remembered the moment I had proposed Anvesha in the Taj vicinity . . . 4 years back.

Then again there was a blast and all the fire went out from the broken building, it seemed like someone was blowing out the fire. It seemed that the building would be saved now. But then suddenly a few seconds later the 2nd huge cylinder hit something and . . .

There came a deafening sound and a blinding light from the Taj Mahal. My TV's speakers had a permanent distortion. The light was so intense that even the LED illuminated display showed a ghost image for over an hour.

A whirlwind started at the place of The Taj Mahal. The sky was overcast, loud thunders started. The whirl sucked in the high up chopper, a loud blast marked the end of whoever was inside it. 2 more choppers were sucked inside it and exploded. The other 6 managed to escape the field.

This thunderstorm continued for the next 30 minutes. Within this time, it engulfed a complete 200km circle, nearly till the border of Delhi. After 10 minutes, their came in reports of an earthquake in Agra which was increasing in intensity every minute. There was dust, terror, tremor, chaos, fear and signs of devastation in peoples head and surroundings. By 5 minutes, the quake had become the most massive in recorded history far. It had completely destroyed Agra and half of the state . . .

Satellite pictures showed the world's largest ever cloud of dust and debris over Uttar Pradesh. For the past 50 years the sky over it was only specked with clouds. The quake continued for 3 hours making it the most massive, destructive and the longest in history of evolution.

It took over 3-4 hours for the massive dust cloud to settle down. A few planes went in to investigate and all that was heard were a couple of explosions and the planes never came out. The sound which came out was reported to be similar to the one of metal striking metal. I was glued to the TV for the complete day for the latest developments. Never before was live TV so interesting enough . . . However the live TV link went off the rock abruptly. All satellite communication went down and feeling helpless I went to sleep . . .

2 hours later. My cell showed 'Anvesha calling . . .'

"Yes beautiful . . . What's up???"

"Did u see what happened in UP???" she squealed into the phone.

"Hey hey! Cool down! I saw it . . . Agra is devastated . . ." I replied.

"Oh you are so not in contact with GK!!! Switch the TV on see it . . . I can't explain it in words . . . U got to see it to believe it . . ."

The way she said that last line was so desperate with enthusiasm that I knew it had to be something . . . I rushed and switched the TV on . . .

I could not believe what I was looking at. The scenes . . . which behold me were undoubtedly the most expensive, unbelievable and the unimaginable site of all ages.

At the site of the Taj Mahal was now the highest mountain in the solar system. At 40 kilometres in height, it was taller than the highest mountain ever known to mankind by more than 10 kilometres. The extent of it below the sea level was another 10 kilometres. The expanse of the mountain totalled nearly 400 kilometres. To add spice to all that, the mountain was surrounded on all sides by a 20km wide crude oil reservoir, this made it wider than the widest river on the planet. Plus, there was one more difference. The biggest difference of all . . . . This naked mountain was of SOLID GOLD and Platinum . . . No wonder the world forgot the Taj.

It could not be seen with a naked eye because of the sunlight reflection nor could it fit in the view of any camera. The greenhouse effect was profound around the mountain. The light scattering effect was such that even the sky took up a golden aura for 100 kilometres from the mountain. And it was the only structure on earth which could be seen clearly from the moon.

India, now, was the richest country in the world by a margin beyond belief.

―――∞∞∞―――

Dr. Pratyush Dhage

This was what was known in the Euphrates scriptures as the 'Treasure of the Gods' or the Doomsday mountain of gold.

Location—BLUECOVER Corp.

The corporation had the privilege of discovering the world's most deadly biological weapon and now . . . the biggest treasure in the universe . . .

Sheemal Jezebeth was on the top of the world. He was now the man in history who had discovered the treasure of a lifetime. Even if he came to limelight as the destroyer of the Taj Mahal, the Indian Government would crush all the protests which would occur anywhere in the world against him.

BLUECOVER Corp was now the world's richest and largest R&D facility for weapons in the world.

"It should be larger and more grand, a bigger place!!" SHEEMAL JEZEBETH thought.

———∞———

A change came over the world economy and attitude, infiltration in India increased by 1000 times from each route, it was a mad rush for gold from every place in the world. Investments increased by 100 folds in the country, homes were sold as diamonds with the view; the whole world looked upon a new economic super power in the New Age. Treasure hunts were launched; all the security measures were failing in front of the human greed for gold. Hordes of people rushed to grab the gold flakes and stones but their boats sunk in the oil and bodies never recovered. Over the period on months, many attempted to reach the gold, but all died. Some sunk in the oil, some were burnt, some went blind, some got seizures, some collapsed, some got heart attacks, but no one was able to touch the gold. From the sky or land no one could reach it, but the hope of greed prevailed that someday the mountain would be conquered. Till then, it just remained as the most beautiful sight of monstrously divine proportions . . .

Back inside my house I switched on the TV. They were showing breaking news. The world's largest arsenal was being built somewhere. All the countries who had a bio-nuclear arsenal were supporting it; the number being 68 of the 195 countries of the world. Such a large amount of money was involved that it was scheduled to be built in 20 days.

'What exactly is going on in this world?' I asked myself and lied down to sleep . . .

Location—Unknown, somewhere in Ladakh, J & K

Work was at full pace for the construction of the BWS. Staggering amounts of money had been put in for its construction. It was being built by the Bluecover Corp. under a fake name. Greater than the GDP of all developed countries was only an indication of the amount which was required for it.

This place was being equipped for the state of the art research facilities for biological weapons worldwide. Protests were on world over to stop the mad race for the weapons; demands of the United Nations were falling on deaf ears. Everyone was now sure of an upcoming World War III and was expecting it to be the most gruesome and barbaric of all wars fought till date on the planet. However in an official meeting of defence heads, like before, it was decided that the use of these weapons would be limited to on militancy, terrorism and never in wars even when the country would be on the verge of losing it. However this was never revealed to the media hence in the neural system was an unknown fear.

The huge construction of the BWS was completed in 19 days, the world's fastest construction of an arsenal till date. The structure was resistant to every force present on the earth. Wireless, wired or natural; nothing could make a scratch on the BWS—not even a neutron bomb . . . It wasn't detectable on satellite maps. During the inauguration of the BWS, defence heads of all the nations were present there. Research was on from the first day itself. There were anti-gravity chambers, vacuum chambers, 10x gravity chambers, ultra fast corpse cutters and others for the ultimate research in everything related to destructive biology and chemistry.

Each country had prepared an anti-weapon to the original. Nearly all had to be administered within 5-10 minutes of coming in contact with the weapon. India too had them for the entire r-DNA tech, but fortunately or unfortunately they could not prepare the anti-weapon to the original VETOX. There isn't a solution to everything . . . always.

Location—Defence HQ, INDIA.

All the heads had assembled with some high source politicians. It was supposed to be a casual meeting to rejoice over BWS, but . . .

"Gentlemen how's your that things going on in that new place?" A man in spotless white clothes asked.

"What that thing?" the IAF chief asked.

"That finding out thing above JK . . ." he said as he picked up an expensive drink.

"Research?" the chief asked.

"Yes yes . . ."

"Superb! Best of all years!"

"Bastard does not know primary school English and he is the defence minister. Asses in white clothes." the Navy chief said to the army chief and laughed over it.

About an hour later, the home minister, finance minister and the defence minister had a small discussion and requested the 3 chiefs to sit at a round table. 6 high profilers along with 4 young officers and 3 secretaries took the total on the table to 13.

"So what's the best weapon you've got, I mean how effective is it?"

"Sir, it's like you see it and you are dead in 30seconds . . . it has a lucid smell which draws you to it, and half an hour later there is only a pool of blood left." The IAF chief said flatly.

"And the worst then?"

"Not the worst but the invincible is still the original." INS chief said.

"What is the total worth of them?" the FM asked.

"North of 1,00,000 crore." All the chiefs said.

"Well then we have a plan, but we want to talk about it alone." The HM said looking at the secretaries and signalled them to go out. Then he asked the chiefs to send the officers out, the officers glanced at the chiefs who gave an affirmative nod. Now there were only 6 people inside.

"Yes, what is it?" The IA chief said.

"See, we all know that you 3 are currently the whole and sole of this research, you know how much power you wield and your value is worth more than diamonds. Even the PM has no idea of this venture of yours."

"How do you know all this?" the 3 asked baffled.

"Leave the details, what I want to say is, we will help you become the most powerful trio in the country who wield power and aura . . . but if you get along with us." The HM said.

"How is that?"

"We, give you each 10,000 crore, and 4000 crore to those outside, all you have to do is keep the forces with us and we can easily take over the government." The DM said.

"Is it so simple?" the IAF chief asked.

"More than that, if all the security is mine then who is going to stop me . . ." the DM said and laughed.

All of the 6 people picked up their glasses and gave big cheers.

"Let's enjoy, the country is now ours!" the HM shouted.

"How will you give the money?" INS chief asked.

"All is ready in cash." FM said.

'People's money . . .' the INS chief said to himself.

"What do we need to do?"

"We just make a deal and the money reaches your home before you do." The FM said.

"And what if we don't?" IAF chief asked as he sat down on the table.

"Then you die and the others get your share." The other 2 chiefs looked at each other.

"We won't be accomplices; you can do whatever you want to." IAF chief said pointing a finger.

The FM had a gun with him; he went close to the chief and fired into his abdomen. "Now you two . . ." the FM turned to the others.

The gunshot brought the other 7 people inside. The young officers had their shiny guns in their hands.

They saw the dead chief and raised their guns at everyone inside.

"They both killed him . . ." the DM shouted pointing to the chiefs and his trouser went wet between the legs.

The young officer fired the bullet straight into the DM's head, the FM took out his gun to fire at him but the other officer behind was quicker and 3 bullets entered the FM's head before his fingers could touch the trigger.

"What about them, sir?" An officer asked waving his gun at the HM and the secretaries as the latter shook in fear.

"Target Practice . . ." the INS chief shouted and laughed.

"Run for your lives . . ." Everyone shouted in unison and the next second 18 bullets roasted the body of the minister and blasted the brains of the secretaries. Their drivers outside were then thrown in the testing wing of Bluecover.

The next day newspapers read—"FM, DM, HM, IAF Chief and 3 others die in plane crash. Bodies missing."

13 people sat at a table, 6 died. The numbers were playing a game—more deadly than ever . . .

Location—BLUECOVER Corp.

All the research was perfect in the labs and now it was the premier place for Biological weapon research. However something was not right . . . There was an undergoing change . . .

A meeting was being held in the most unknown portion of the labs—The DOME.

As the name states, it was a super-strength glass dome surrounded on all sides by heavy water. A treadmill or a flat escalator was the only entry to it. The heavy water surrounding it was drained before and after any to be held meeting to allow entry and exit. After those in the meeting would enter the dome, it was closed and heavy water would be poured. The watertight chamber could hold up to 1,00,000 litres of heavy water around it and withstand the pressure. It took 5 minutes to fill and 10 minutes to empty. No sound could escape from the chamber and it could hold 25 people inside it on couches. To keep the meetings a complete secret, no one ever knew that the air which was pumped in was mixed with 2 special gases—Apathy Gas and M-Clear. These made sure that no one opposed and no-one ever recalled what happened inside. But there was something wrong, and the creators of the gases had an antidote for them. It was only with Sheemal Jezebeth and a few other people. Generally these were the only people who called the meetings.

After the high profile meeting which had only 4 people including Sheemal Jezebeth, a weird notice was circulated among the 25 high post people of the Labs. It said-

"DOME—National Security"

Location—DR. AVNIKA's House.

The sporty car screeched into the basement of the 20 floored building which had only one residence per floor. A young man and woman got down. They press 20 inside the ultra high speed elevator which takes them to DR. Avnika's residence in just 5 seconds. They press the doorbell. Avnika is in her study chamber. Dejectedly she gets up and presses a button on the LED display which activates the camera at her door. The display shows the two faces seeing which her face lights up.

"Cool . . . Anik and Kelly." She chirps and presses the ALLOW button on the interface which unlocks the door with a click.

"Hi lovebirds . . ." Avnika says as she hugs them both.

"So Avni how's life?" Kelly asks her.

"Great, a bit relaxed now."

"Why not, you are now the head of Forensic Genetics the Lab." Anik said

"You and your silly lab! No one knows where it is and how it is . . . My gynaecology clinic is better." Kelly said.

"It sure is dear . . ." Anik winked and said. "Oh shut up!" Kelly fakely slapped Anik and entered the Relaxing room.

"Listen I've got something important to talk about." Anik said seriously.

"Just wait for a minute!" Avnika said and rushed to her kitchen. There was a sound of the microwave and she came out with 2 mugs of piping hot coffee.

"Yes, now say!"

"Please take it seriously whatever I'm going to say!" Anik said with a grim expression.

"Hmmmm ok . . ."

"2 days back in the cybernetic research lab I overheard 2-3 people talking about takeover, defence, killing, government and like that."

"So what these things are very common in our labs and especially your section is always ready with these things, isn't it?" Avnika said stone-faced as she crossed her legs.

"No it's not like that, the government thing seems scandalous, and the talk was more sinister." Anik protested.

"Stop watching all those war movies will you! Your mind is full with those stories." Avnika flouted all his observations and requests.

"You don't understand, listen to this." Anik took out his virtual surround playback device and switched it on.

"WE %$%A%RE AT THE MO%&ST %$SECURE%^$&%^$ EST%^$*(ABL342IS8O79HMENT IN INDIA. THE IAF CH&^%IEF, DEFEN#%$*CE, FIN#@@$CE AND HOYO87362806ME MI%NI$#$STERS HAVE B$EEN KIL*(^&*)^LED BY OUR F!@!#$ INDI#%$*RECTLY723652605 THE A%&^)RMY HAS MA^*)*(DE IT E&^&%^ASY FO76697R US, NO*W WE8398 NEED TO !@#$%^&(*&^% ARMY AND NAVY !@#$%^&^%$ TO TAK^&%^*&%EOVER AND #$%^&^%$# GOV%%$$#"

"What does all this mean, in line with what we all know, all these were killed in an accidental plane crash, but this thing was planned in our labs. Doesn't it reveal a different face of the place where we work?" Anik had a helpless expression on his face.

"Where did you get that all from?" Avnika said.

"I hacked this from the cybertron hotlink server of our labs just because I heard those words."

"It's not properly audible; let me listen to it for a while clearly." Avnika plugged in the Grado's lying on the table into the device. She played it 3 times and finally got to grips, her facial expression changed now.

"This is Grade Z matter." Avnika said.

"So you get now?"

"But Bluecover has an encryption system in the server, right?"

"That's the reason everything is so garbled up and unclear." Anik said.

"Are you sure that it was the same thing, you could have mixed up 2 or more conversations?" Avnika put forward a doubt.

"Rare chance, the guy speaking is the same throughout, listen to it once more; don't you think you know the voice . . . ?" Anik said.

"Kind of yes, seems so that I have heard this voice many times and quite recently on the television also I suppose. Whose is it?"

"It is Sheemal Jezebeth!" Anik said quietly.

"Hmmm, then you might be true also. He was too enthusiastic over VETOX also. He is a freak in total. Bluecover is a complete tangle." Avnika finally agreed.

"So finally . . ." Anik hushed.

"What's on your mind over that thing?"

"I will need your help."

"irt what?" Avnika said.

"For the meeting, inside The DOME . . ."

"Come again . . ." Avnika flashed.

"I need your help. We need to know what is going on inside the Dome. No one remembers anything about what went on inside the chamber when they come out."

"Are you out of your mind? You cannot take anything, any outside material except the clothes on your body inside. What do want me to take inside, this funny recorder of yours???" Saying this, Avnika threw the recorder to Anik back.

"No we can place it on you . . ."

"The dome has octa-level of scan, it sometimes points out to the metal content of the nail polish, do you know that?" she placed a query.

"I know, but it has one inherent weakness, it cannot go more than 2mm in case the material is enclosed in crystalline calcium more than 10times the density of bone!"

"And where do you expect to find such a kind of calcium?? I have to go bare handed inside." She said with a blank expression.

"In your mouth . . ." Anik flashed.

"Whattttttttttttt????????????" she was surprised.

"Yes, Anvesha told me when she was in her 2nd year, that teeth are 10 times denser than bone and have a crystalline structure."

"You are born for cybernetics man!!" Avnika said as she gave Anik a patting on his shoulder.

"Give me that model." Anik said pointing to the molar model in the showcase. "It'll give me some idea, and I can always get the real dimensions from Anvi."

Location—Dr. Anvesha's house.

The super tuned car raced in to the bungalow compound and the car dashingly stopped as Anik pulls the handbrake while the steering is completely turned left.

He walks inside to Dr. Anvesha's room where he finds her studying on the bed.

"Hi miss cute doctor!" Anik said as Anvesha closed the book . . .

"Hi hacker!" Anvesha said.

"Don't call me hacker, I'm not one." Anik protested.

"But you can be a great one."

"Ok fine. Every time you say that I have no reply to the truth." Anik laughs and says.

"Sooooo . . . how come here today?"

"Do you have a tooth to show me?"

"Ya, sure." Saying this Anvesha took out a clean tooth from a box on her table.

"It looks so nice. Which is it?" Anik said.

"It is a lower molar tooth; I extracted it around 15 days back. I've cleaned it thoroughly afterwards. You can hold it with your bare hands, fear not."

"I wanted to know something in dental treatment."

"What What What???" Anvesha flashed eagerly.

"Hey cool down miss, tell me is there any treatment in which we hollow out the tooth?"

"Yes, from ages . . . , we call it endodontic treatment." Anvesha said.

"Eh . . . ??? Err . . . !! What actually do you do in it?"

"See, we enter the tooth from the top or bottom depending on whether it is a lower or upper tooth, and then with the help of excavators and micro-files we remove the live tissue inside the chamber."

"Do you mean to say there is a hollow empty space inside the tooth?" Anik said with a sparkle.

"Yes, but you can't keep that empty, we fill it up with an artificial nerve till the end so that the infection does not re-enter the tooth."

"How does the tissue inside the tooth remain alive? As far as I know you need blood and nerves to keep a tissue alive; and this tooth seems to be closed from all sides." Anik said as he saw the tooth from all sides.

"There are microscopic entry pores at the tip of the root around .3 to .4mm in diameter. When we do the treatment these pores are widened to a macroscopic level. The blood and nerve come through these pores only. The main nerve is just approx 2-3mm below the root tip, which supplies a

70mv of power to the tissue." Anvesha went simple explaining the story.

"Enough it seems . . ." Anik mumbled to himself. "What did you say?" Anvesha asked bouncing her eyebrows.

"Nothing nothing, How much time does all this take?" Anik queried.

"Depends, but in ideal conditions without any complications 35-40minutes."

"Which tooth is this?" Anik said showing the dummy model.

"Hey, this is from Yash's clinic, did you get it from him?"

"No no, from Avni!" "O, OK." Anvesha chipped.

"Hacker, this is the Mandibular first molar."

"Tell me something more about inside it, in way that I can understand. And are there any fixed dimensions of each tooth?" He chirped.

Anvesha inserted a BluRay disc of her course book inside her funky laptop. She showed him a normal tooth and an endodontically treated tooth. Anik looked at the latter with great interest.

"You can get the average dimensions from the measurements section; each tooth even of the same type has different dimensions even in the same mouth. Specific scans can tell you the exact dimensions."

"Cool, thanks; can I have this tooth and the disc?" Anik said as he got up.

"All yours, sweetie hacker." Anvesha said as she gave him a parting hug and a Mandibular 1st molar of the right side.

———∞∞∞———

Date—3 November

I was getting ready to go when I saw the multicoloured led on my cell flickering. It showed "Avnika"

Hi doc? What's up and how was your engagement? She asked

"Heh heh . . ." I giggled.

"Man you blush a lot . . . First boy I've seen who blushes so much.

I got my leg pulled by miss super intello.

"Ok now, when are u free, I need an appointment." She said

"You people are vvvvvip's, you don't need silly appointments".

"But we need some extra free time . . ." She said

"Anytime maam, come in the afternoon. I said.

"Ok at 2 then. Byeee. And one thing more . . ."

"What?" I said quietly.

"Don't tell Anvesha!"

It was the first day of the week. I finished up most of the cases fast, so that I could be free. I stepped into the outside world to have a chat with Anvi. I had a 40-50 minute love talk with my darling during the break time. It was the first time we talked so much. She did not like chatting on telephone and nor did I. In fact I felt sleepy when the counter crossed 35 and she slept before it crossed 30.

At around 2:10pm an orange car pulled in near. Avnika and Anik got down. "Hey where are your tuned beasts . . . ?" I asked.

"Resting in their caves! This one's the latest addition to our fleet after yours . . ." Avnika said.

"Hmmm." I had a laugh.

We went inside and Avnika sat on the dental chair.

"My tooth is paining . . ."

"Which?" I asked picking up a mouth mirror.

"Ummmm . . . . Mandibular first molar of the right side."

"Anvesha's friend . . ." I thought.

"You don't even have incipient caries!!!" I said after looking and tapping her tooth.

"Doc, we need an endodontic treatment of that tooth." Anik said.

"But it's perfectly all right."

"We need to place this inside it. It's very important!" Anik said and took out a box of the size of an iPod Shuffle.

"This box???" I cracked a joke. Well I only got the joke.

The box had a translucent display on it. Anik placed a part of his palm on the display and removed it 2 seconds later.

A brilliant blue light came out of it and projected on the rotating fan as PALMPRINT ACCEPTED then clicked open.

Inside, placed on a piece of polystyrene was the weirdest thing I had seen in my life. It hideously resembled the pulp structure of a tooth.

"What is it?" I asked big eyes

"This is the newest type of artificial pulp for a first molar."

"It's not, tell me what it is?" I was dumb big eyes.

"It's the world's smallest, most advanced and concealed voice capturing device." Anik said.

"Oh! That's so sci-fi." I chipped like a child presented with an éclairs.

"See doc we have to place it in her molar. You need to hollow out the tooth till the nerve and place this. It's really important." Anik said it seriously.

I injected the local anaesthetic and proceeded with endodontic treatment, did the tooth preparation according to his requirement keeping more than 2mm layer of crystalline calcium and hollowing out the tooth and bone until the nerve supplying the jaw and tooth could be reached. It took over 50 minutes for preparing the tooth for greater than implant length.

"Here now, place this doc!" Anik saw the 4 wide canals in the molar and picked up the artificial pulp with his plastic tweezers.

As he picked it up, a fluorescent red light blinked twice and went off. From the lower portion out came 4 tail like structures in the same configurations as of the 4 root canals. All 4 tails had some kind of rotary clutchers at their ends.

"What are those things?" I asked big eyes again.

"These are the power source explorers." Anik said.

"So?" I asked.

When you place them inside the tooth, these will go through the created path and lock on to the inferior nerves neural sheath." Avnika explained.

"Thus, getting a never ending power source for the device." Anik said.

"But it will pain terribly when that thing will clutch the nerve." I exclaimed.

"This is Grade 7 Bio-Compatible CARBON-FIBRE with Titanium admixed Technetium. The neural sheath will get used to it in a few hours, at the max 3! Now no more questions doc, place this device before it runs out of its internal power reserve." Anik said as he moved his ring over its top surface. This time a green light flicked again, the mechanism at its exploring tips rotated at the max speed.

"Will it calm down?" I asked as I took the thing from Anik's hand.

"Not until it finds the nerve . . ."

"Well then." I carefully took the thing to her molar and those claws quietly went inside the tooth preparation. The device snugly fitted inside the tooth. A minute or so later Avnika shouted and jumped in the chair. Anik said, "Yessssssssss!" and my mental stress shot up like in a heart attack.

"Wh . . . . wh . . . . what happened?" I asked as I lost my grip on the tweezers.

"Don't worry doc! It just confirms the Latching of the Neural Sheath; nothing to worry now!" Anik said triumphantly and showed the LED which blinked rhythmically.

"Are you sure?" I asked fearfully.

"No tension doc! Anyways we had done a sectional CT of the tooth and MRI of the supporting structures, there was a very little chance that we could go wrong with the device." Avnika squeezed my hand and said.

Anik gave me a micro-perforated tooth contoured crystalline calcium resin sheet which I placed over the device and the tooth to let sound waves in.

When the job was finished, It was nearly 4pm. Anik told me that it could record even if placed in a bucket full of Mercury and withstand the pressure for 10 seconds. It would filter out Avnika's voice due to its high intensity. Avnika was just required to keep her mouth open to let the sound clearly in.

To switch on and off the recording, she was required to bite hard on something by that tooth for 1 sec. The device had 7 TB of memory, Anik told me.

———— ∞∞ ————

Location—The DOME, Bluecover Corp.

The platinum door of the dome slid open as the treadmill came out of the glass enclosure. The interior of the dome was infused with Apathy and M-clear.

All the 25 people had assembled at the dome and stepped on the flat escalator. Everyone was in their 40's, but only a few were in their 20's; DR. Avnika was one of them. The meeting started.

A man in black apron sitting near Sheemal Jezebeth got up and went to the center stage.

"Friends, today we are working arguably at the most powerful, advanced and hyper-technology institute of the world. You all are of the caliber which is not found in 99% of the humans. For this purpose you deserve an eminent place in this country, you are not meant to be ruled over you need to rule over." And then he stopped speaking. No one was able to make any head or tail of the few lines he had said. Then he called another person on to the stage.

"As I know, he is our head at the Bluecover Corp Nuclear Wing. He would further elaborate on what I said."

"Let me come to the point straight. I was formerly the Head of operations at BARC, Mumbai. I've worked there since Bhabha's death. You can call BARC as the biggest strength or the biggest weakness of the city."

Sheemal Jezebeth got up. "We've thought about and formulate to put in action, a never before thought about plan which will utilize the biggest weakness of the business capital of the country. We plan to take over the Atomic Research Centre and then the government of the state. The current head of operations is here with us and is all ready to co-operate with us in this regard. All we need are the 25 palm prints on the electronic chronicle so that we can instantly start with the takeover." He said as he held hands with the man in the black apron.

With these thoughts of revolution the meeting at the Dome came to an end. Why it was termed as National Security was still an unanswered question . . .

Location—DR. Avnika's Residence, The same evening.

The car screeched into the parking and the lift takes Anik to the 20th floor in 5 seconds. Avnika is lying in her relaxing room with the room LED's glowing on and off amidst the hazy green ambience lights. As the enormous display shows who is on the door, she gets up and shuts down the devices in the room.

With the normal greetings over, Anik opens his weird congruence device and gives a chewing gum to Avnika. "Hey keep biting this." The device connects wirelessly to the voice capturing device.

Anik played the clip and both of them listened it to in amazement and sheer horror. It was not a simple plan or a revolution but the one which was planned and would be carried out by some of the most powerful and equipped minds of the country.

"If they have BARC in their hands, there's no one who can stop them. Even the central government will have to kneel down. If they threaten the government to blow it up the president and the prime minister have no other option but to listen to them. If they blow up BARC, they blow up the country's money within 2minutes. Neither can the government attack it nor can it ignore. Either way the government can't avoid a holocaust." Anik said.

"It's not that easy . . ." Avnika said, but Anik knew by previous incidents that the freaks at the labs would not even give a second thought over doing any action. If they could not lay their hands on it, they would not let anyone enjoy it anymore.

"What can we do?" Anik asked. Avnika was lost in her thoughts standing near the glass door.

"Hey . . . wake up . . ." Anik said loud.

"There's nothing we can do . . . understand . . . ! We don't own Bluecover, we work there, and we are bloody servants. Get that in your pigmy head. There is only one way. We quit and shift elsewhere. Got it in your head . . ." Avnika screamed at him and slammed the toughened glass door so hard that it ended up in smithereens.

Location—Nuclear division, Bluecover Corp.

A nuclear reactor was proposed to be closed by December 2010 at BARC, but the Bluecover Corp under the name of BWS acquired it and opened it for internal research. Since no maintenance had been done after the shutdown, the Nuclear Division revamped it for research. They independently created the nuclear weapon of the mixed variety Fission + Fusion and it wasn't impossible.

Internally now the head of operations of the Nuclear Division at the BWS, Bluecover and at BARC was the same. The BARC was now completely under the control of Bluecover Corp. they bribed everyone related and on December 1 came out with a deadly warning on the media for the President and PM.

"WE HOLD THE NERVE . . . IT WOULD ONLY TAKE A MATTER OF MINUTES FOR THE POLITICAL MAP OF THIS COUNTRY TO CHANGE.

ONLY A MATTER OF MINUTES TO SEE ON THE STREETS—A CONSORTIUM OF BLOOD

ONLY A FEW MINUTES TO DETHAW EACH BONE IN THE CITY

AND JUST 2 MINUTES, TO SEE A SAHARA REPLACE MUMBAI.

PAY HEED, DECIDE QUICKLY, BECAUSE THIS TIME;

NO HASTE WILL MAKE WASTE"

There was chaos everywhere. It seemed that the think portion of everyone was shutdown on that day.

Hordes of cars, trucks, bikes made a beeline for the city exit roads. Prices skyrocketed, humanity lost its face, and there started riots at the most places. The situation was horrifying, every place of interest was closed, hotels, hospitals, clinics, showrooms were ransacked and broken down. The entire dental clinic's present citywide closed. 'Teeth are not important when life was involved.' People considered general stores a part of life and those places did not remain general anymore. The people who did not leave the city avoided coming out on roads. The most powerful city of India was now at the mercy of those who ran it, however everything had not stopped; the high class still went on with business.

On December 4, a group of people shut down the Dalaal Street—They were from BARC, and that was the first day in 200 years when the city which never blinked whether terrorists attacked or came floods or cyclones, riots or for the matter widespread fires, closed its eyes and one of the world's fastest cities came to a grinding halt. Bank accounts were emptied at speeds faster than light. Banks were only rooms of concrete and metal.

I looked out of the window; it was depressing kind of an atmosphere everywhere. Everyone around was jobless. Future was just a blank. Even the telecom networks had gone off the air. It seemed like the pre 1999 era when there were no mobiles.

In this entire wilderness, I saw Anvi's car as it turned into my house gate. It was like a ray of joy for me. Anvesha's friends stepped out of the car. Anvesha looked lovely but sad. Avni and Anik wanted to talk to my parents. I went to the roof with Anvi.

Anvesha place her elbow on the edge and rested her chin on her palm and looked around. There was silence everywhere and the roads were empty. I looked at her as a tear tried to trickle down her right cheek. I held it with my finger.

"Don't cry sweetheart. Everything will be ok soon . . ."

"No nothing's going to be ok. Everything's finished, nothing's in place anymore." She blurted.

I looked up at the sky for a few seconds. "There are 2 things that will not change ever." She turned towards me, "Huh??"

"The sky up and the thing between you and me . . ." I said as I held her hand. She stepped closer to me. I held her face in my hands.

"You don't look good with your depressed face. Your smile is like a life spray for all those around you. Things may change forever dear but not for any reason will my feeling for you change. You were the princess of my heart from the day I saw you and in the coming days you will be the queen of it."

I took my hands of her face and looked into her eyes. There was something going on in her mind. Of all the faces I could never read hers.

She placed one of her hand on my shoulder and the other on my neck, pulled my face close and tactfully placed my lower lip between hers and sucked it hard. It was equivalent to 10 intra cardiac shots at a time.

Her lips were so soft, I hugged her tight, and she stepped on to my feet and dug her nails deeper into my hair and shoulder. We were as close as we could be on an evening on a roof. I lifted her up and took her to the railing as our moments of passion entered the 39th minute.

Seconds later, I heard Avnika clearing her throat. A thought ran through my mind, 'The worst sound one can hear during kissing is someone clearing his or her throat.'

We left each other in a fraction of a second as Avnika said, "Doctors!" we looked at each other.

"Fiery moment of yours, sorry to spill water over it . . ." Avnika continued in her own style. It would be hard to find her a boy.

"What happened?" Anvi popped.

"Well I convinced everyone to leave the city. Next week we'll leave. I have booked farmhouses for all of us; these things have lost value like anything. All the better for us to help in starting a new life . . ." Avnika said as she looked up at the sky. This was the first time I saw her like this. It would not be hard finding her a boy.

Anvi went to Avni to give her a happy hug and whispered into her ear. Avnika winked and went back downstairs. Anvesha and I talked a lot that evening; from the day we first met till the 5 minute back kiss. A kind of time travel, through our love life. Those were the days when everything was running and no one was concerned. In the end we kissed again.

1 week later . . .

It was 5 in the morning when my dad shook me up for the day. "Get up, we have to leave today." He said.

I went around with the normal morning routine with a neutral kind of feeling in my brain. I did not know whether to be happy or sad. I did not know what was going to happen next . . . since all wireless devices (read Mobile phones) had gone off air a month before, I called Avnika, Anvesha and Anik once from the landline. They told me to wait at the biggest highway crossroads of the state near a police station; if it existed any more. Law in the country had collapsed faster than a controlled detonation building would . . .

I and my parents were in separate cars. An hour or so later I was near the cross roads, the whole area was devastated. The police station was covered with flies and it was stinking. Outside the building were lying a few chopped portions of the human body with crows feeding on them. The stars on the ripped khaki uniforms lay on the blood stained grass. 'Rajesh . . .' said the name on the broken nameplate. I shuddered on seeing such a scene and stopped the car half a kilometer ahead of the location. About 50 minutes later the 3 cars arrived and stopped near ours.

There were not much chats, we were to plainly follow the navigation instructions in our cars. Anvesha's mom and dad had also come; they however had a small chat with my parents. Anvesha's car like everybody else's was packed with luggage and she was having a weird time sitting cramped on the rear seat. She hopped into my car. Needless to say, I was more than happy.

We started the journey. Nature had not changed a bit even though the city was lifeless; our surroundings were abounding with greenery. We decided to stop every 1-2 hours to stock up food and fuel though we had enough of both. We had to reach the spot before sunset. It was our journey to a presumed safety and security. On the way we saw the warehouses which had been ransacked and destroyed by miscreants in the past few days. Avnika, Anik n Kelly, Me, my parents and finally

Anvesha's parents was the sequence in the on road journey. Her father was too mild as compared to her.

Inside the car we talked and observed a lot. We maintained a triple digit average speed because there was no one on the roads except stray dogs and cattle. Like the good old days. All the luggage movers either had been abandoned due to lack of fuel or accidents. Many of them were lying on the highway upturned or just like that with tons of blood splashes on them. The whole drive was turning out to be a fearful experience. We saw a heavily guarded fuel outlet, no one was allowed out of the vehicles when on or near the outlet. Anyone who would step out would invariably be killed without a warning. Situation worldwide was degrading faster than food kept in the open. I tried to keep those thoughts away and started a conversation with my darling.

"So dear what's up your mind?" she turned towards me and rested herself on the door. I swiftly double checked the lock.

"Shoo shweet . . ." she chipped and switched off the A/C as she pressed the window down button and said "Morning fresh air." A gust of air flowed inside playing her hair over her face and some over mine. She looked enticingly gorgeous. I reduced the speed as she poked her head out of the window. She took a few deep breaths and came inside. After 7 hours of continuous travel we stopped near a stream. After confirming that it was safe we got down from the cars and stretched ourselves out.

"Avoid the stream." Avnika said to all of us. "Why is she saying so?" I asked in Anvi's ear and in reply she also showed me the same question mark on her face.

"It's not that stream!" Anik said to her hushing tones. Everyone else was just looking at them, and by that time Anvesha, Kelly and I had stepped in the water. "Why the hell are you stepping in the water . . . ?" Avnika screamed at us. We froze in the water as we heard her scream. I had never seen her in such a mood before.

Anik tried to control her, "Avni, get over your senses, it's not what you are thinking. You are just getting apprehensive . . ." he held her as she fell in his arms as her body lost tone.

"No, I'm not wrong, look there upstream." She pointed and all the eyeballs rolled the same direction. We saw a human lying with his hand in the water. Anik's face turned pale as he saw the being. "Why are you two talking like this? Is the water poisoned? But how do you know? How can you tell?" Kelly went berserk looking at the chaos. Our faces too went pale, 'Were we doomed? I asked myself.

Anik picked up a stone and threw it near the body. "What are you doing?" Anvesha asked him scared.

"He moved, I think . . ." I said in Anvesha's ear. She looked at me. Her face had never been so pale in life.

Anik did it once more, "Don't do it!" Kelly choked and everyone made a dash out of water.

Anik picked up another stone and hurled it, maybe anxiety and fear was getting the better of him.

"Hey stop throwing those stones idiots." Someone shouted. We turned and in front of our eyes, that so called body got up and said. He was around 25 years and in tattered clothes. We all let out a sigh of relief. He walked to us and told about himself.

We learnt that he was a victim of human trafficking, something happened on the way to Mumbai. A group of people broke the truck with their weird weapons and literally split open everyone killing and massacring everyone in the truck. He was the lone survivor of the homicide because he managed to run away and hide inside the water. We shuddered on listening the story and dashed in to our cars to get on. Before 7PM we had to reach the spot or the man who was supposed to meet us would leave. Property rates had anti rocketed after the shutdown. Anik requested our parents to drive faster and put pedal to metal, and we all did that.

Everybody's mood changed to good on the way as the time passed. We were now looking forward to reach our new houses. At an average speed of 140kmph we made it to the destination by around 6:50PM. We all had a great time playing fake races, made fake faces when someone lost, and cheered the person who won. In all, those 3 hours were the best time we had spent in the past 10 desolate days.

The man was waiting for us as we reached the place. "I had lost hope of you all coming, but you proved me wrong." He said with a beaming face. "Here are the keys to the 6 bungalows . . ." He handed the keys to Avnika and left in his car.

"We are 5 families, what for is the 6th key?" I asked myself in my mind and a few seconds Avni answered my question with my eyes.

She dangled the keys in front of Anvesha and Me, and winked at us. "Coool . . ." I said.

"Till that time they are gonna be with me . . . !" Avni said as Anvesha stealthily bit me on my shoulder. She was on cloud nine.

We went to our respective bungalows. It was not much of a job setting up the house, everything was already present inside. An hour or so later I switched on the TV. Private channels had gone off air, only the National Network was on air.

On Anvesha's birthday and December 14 the news was special. The government had loosened its hold on the issue and gave the control of Mumbai to BARC. Armed intervention had been no use because, the batch which went inside the BSE were thrown out after half an hour and post mortem studies showed 1 cm thrombi in the meningeal vessels.

On December 15, BSE resumed function with a terrified heart. Within a week or so, everything related to business was back on tracks. BARC lifted all taxes for a period of 15 years. Toll booths, the thing for which Mumbai is infamous throughout the world were shut down permanently. Political parties no more existed; all the administrative buildings were rid of uneducated politicians. It all seemed too good to be true but it was a reality today. 'Was it an everlasting peace and hope or was it the deathly silence before a tornado? 'I pondered.

Location—Nuclear Div, BWS.

"Guys, we broke the spine of India. I did not expect it to be so easy!" Sheemal Jezebeth said.

"Sir, if we throw some more money, we can overpower the central govt too . . . Anyways we hold the brain of the country . . ." the head of operations of BARC said, and moved his fingers in his non-existent hair on his head and laughed.

"Yes, that's the next stage of our operation; I'm studying the security stages of the president's house, parliament, and the 3 defence heads . . ."

"What would be a tentative date???"

"Christmas" Sheemal Jezebeth laughed and said.

"All the places at once?"

"Yes, and now I'll get the cybernetic wing of BLUECOVER ready." Sheemal Jezebeth picked up his black blazer, tossed it over his shoulder and left for the communication centre. It would now be done at an emergency scale.

Location—Cybernetic division, BLUECOVER Corp.

A streaming communication device rang with all its glory and the projector displayed

"BWS NUCLEAR DIVISION"

Someone present answered the call.

Sheemal Jezebeth started,

"Nuclear division on its heels now . . . We fear no one. Gear up for a Fusion assault on NEW DELHI. 25th December . . . We reign India.

There was a technique to detonate the bomb via a satellite however in addition; BLUECOVER had perfected a weird technique of 'AM signal detonation.' This made sure that in the worst possible situation too, the bomb would detonate. They now just had to place the death piece at the proper place on Christmas.

———◦∞◦———

Mumbai finally resumed function. Everything including the cell phone services was back on line. Everyone was kind of happy. I too was to reopen my clinic. Avnika and Anik planned to get back to their jobs. In all that chaos Anvesha too had been given all her completion certificates in haste. So before all this, we planned to go for a 10-15 day picnic cum New Year vacation. Now the question was where to go . . . so finally we set out for the picnic on 17 December. No specific location was decided and we were to explore places as we came upon them in our 700km picnic. Defy normal that's what we had decided.

The days clicked past, we were a happy lot; there were no limits to ecstasy. As the days went by, we explored the still untouched parts of India; stopping here and there we covered only 150kms average every day. It was fun in two cars, Avnika's and mine.

On 23 December, we stopped at a dedicated camping site somewhere in Madhya Pradesh. After setting up our tents and a bonfire we laughed, danced, shouted, screamed, ran, jumped, did all FUN things that people call BEING MAD. At 3Am or so we sat down exhausted in front of the still burning bonfire, few minutes later the girls went in to their tents and I and Anik stayed back. The fire died down 15 minutes later and Anik went inside tent. I kept lying down looking at the sky it seemed so peaceful, so unlike the earth. I did not feel like sleeping in the tent so I unloaded some of the luggage from my car and lied down in it and stared at the sky again through the sunroof. Somehow I never felt sleepy on outings.

Something moving outside grabbed my attention. I saw something move in the grass, it was black in color. In the bright moon light it increased in size towards my car and sacred the shit out of me. Seconds later I realized that it was a shadow . . . 'But of what?????' I asked myself I could see thick thread like structures in the shadow. After all the TV seen in the year, one could easily believe in ghosts and evil. I slammed the hatch and sunroof shut and quietly huddled inside the car.

I heard something scratch and struggle at my door. My sweating increased like anything. Then a struggle with the driver door latch. I did not dare to look the window lest the thing see me inside. Then suddenly my phone vibrated hard inside my pocket. I jumped up with fear. LED flickering violet. I answered the phone,

"Yes . . . . wh . . . . What?" I tried to chip.

"What are you doing?" Anvesha said a bit irritated.

"Keep inside the tent, there's something devilish out here, outside my car . . ."

"There's nothing outside and how dare you call me a devil." She scolded me loudly.

"No, really, it's trying to come inside my car!" I chipped a bit clearly.

"Open the hatch will you? The devil's name is Dr. Anvesha! See . . ." she knocked the windscreen, jumped on the bonnet and flashed her illuminated phone screen.

I quickly switched on the cabin light and opened the hatch door and she came inside. We left the hatch open.

"Whattt were you doing just now? Talking in sleep or what?" she asked me.

"I thought that a ghost had come."

"Reallllllly . . . ???????" she asked me cutely and warmly. And seconds later burst out laughing like a cute lunatic as I turned red with embarrassment. Laughing she held my face between her hands and kissed me many times on my face. "Love you . . ."

she said many times and I replied "Love you too . . ." the same number of times.

We were so close to each other, I held her by the waist and dragged her close, moved my hand over her face, and took my lips close to hers. I could feel her mint breath and see the passion on her face. I pressed my lips below her ear and gave her a deep wet and passionate kiss for 15 minutes. She returned it with a superb smooch for the next hour. I don't know when we fell asleep but when we got up she had her head on my chest.

On 25th of December we decided to move ahead. At 0930hrs we started packing up. We had the FM radios of the cars switched on. When I got up in the morning my cell phone did not work meaning that the signal strength was full but the communication was down. An hour or so later the radio went off air.

We left for our next stop; Jabalpur via Seoni. We entered Seoni at 1PM or so; it was completely life less with no activity at all. We wanted to stop for lunch but I saw something horrendous and scary, many doors which were completely splattered with fresh blood and there was a decapitated corpse lying in a narrow lane. We did not dare stop at that place and made a high speed exit from the town.

At 2:30PM the FM radio resumed and the news we heard had taken the world by storm. It said that some armed people had taken the 3 defence heads and the President hostage to somewhere unknown. Some also had taken control of the parliament during its emergency session. They warned, rather, promised to blow up the parliament within 72hours if the central government was not given under their control. They added a line—Remember Mumbai, we are the same.

Nobody knew who these people were and who was funding these operations. Terrorism was wrecking havoc all over India.

Location—Cybernetic division, BLUECOVER Corp.

The PM along with other senior officials of defence flew to the BLUECOVER Labs. With such a volatile situation at hand, the officials had to expose the secret of the labs. The PM was requested not to let out the secret.

The PM was surprised to see the defence spokesperson Sheemal Jezebeth before him at cybernetics.

"Must be prepared for more . . ." he said to himself.

The situation was so out of control that he gave BLUECOVER the responsibility of clearing the mess in the country. Little did he know that he had legalized a new game of deception . . .

Sheemal Jezebeth went inside his chamber. He looked at himself in the mirror, picked up a open wad of notes threw it up in the air looked up at the flying pieces and laughed loud as a shower of currency fell on him.

"India . . . Here I come . . ." he laughed loudly.

They did not need fusion now. The nerve was now under his power and will. BLUECOVER was ready to play a game of horrifying proportions. Sheemal Jezebeth ordered the PM and other officials to be taken underground and bombs focussed at them.

Inborn terrorism had played havoc with India, every place had been involved. The crime rate which had gone down by 90% shot up at double the rate, law had collapsed completely. The place which was once the adobe of gods was now a devils playground. Killings, murders, ever unimagined crimes, homicides, genocides were getting common. Everything known or unknown was being used against everyone. Only far-flung areas were untouched. It was only a matter of time before they would be involved . . . .

People had lost faith—in others, friends, relatives, themselves and the DIVINE . . .

It was the same condition worldwide. The thing which had started in India had spread to the world. The path which the world had taken to was a single lane one way. There was no coming back. If you stopped, you were run over. It was a race towards never ending darkness . . . . It was a race to the ultimate truth, a race to DEATH . . .

Location—BWS.

There was a moment of celebration at the BWS. The aim of the nuclear wing had been achieved, now they had to wait for the government's response or blow up the parliament with everyone inside it.

However, suddenly the BWS shook with a force very strong, its intensity never felt before in history. The whole foundations and the building shook; windows, doors, escalators, radiation protection chambers, nuclear bunkers shattered like anything. Within 5 seconds, millions of billions involved in infrastructure were converted to piles. The security system of BWS which was supposedly the strongest and safest in the world was destroyed in a matter of seconds.

The central roof of BWS was a dome of diamond, resting on 5 pillars of super-reinforced titanium of 3 Feet diameter and 40 feet length. 5 seconds later the roof came crashing down on the ceramo-concrete floor and the titanium pillars crumbled like cardboard.

Everyone inside tried to escape, but each entrance had been blocked by the rubble; everyone made a desperate rush to the central hall. There was one tunnel exit which was only reachable by the entrance at the centre.

The diamond dome landed on the floor as a heap of jewels. A total of 4300 people had gathered; the high rank officials to the cleaner everyone was present.

The diamonds glowed in the dusk, seconds later a mind-soul piercing cry was heard from the open top. Everyone looked up and the scene they saw was one of the most hideous views in the history of mankind.

A very large eagle, the size of a small plane, flew over the top. It circled the BWS once. There was a white egg like shape in its claws which glowed brighter than the sun. The room was now filled with a bright light. The eagle looked down into BWS. Yellow beams came out of its eyes which fell on the diamonds. Those surprisingly glowed red and filled the room now, with a mysterious red glow. The eagle let out a scream which was nerve wrecking as well as frightening that everyone turned pale. The eagle dropped the so called egg on to the heap of diamonds. Everyone looked in terror as the small egg sized thing increased in size rapidly. 10 seconds later, it was over 12 feet in size. It was so bright that it dazzled the eyes of every one there.

Seconds later the brightness decreased and people could make out an outline of a face in it. The face had an angry expression.

The brightness again increased indefinitely and seconds later all the people standing there went blind. Moments later those people heard the last sound If their lives—A hypersonic screech which tore their ear drums and what followed it was an explosion which had 1000 times the energy of nuke.

The explosion was so fast, tremendous and devastating that in 15 seconds it vaporized everything in a demarcated circle of radius 200km. Each and every satellite automatically focussed to the spot. The light emitted from the explosion was so bright that it lit up the dark side of the moon for 15 seconds. The devastation was widespread; everything had disappeared in a circle of 400kms whose center was the BWS. All that remained was shiny granite.

BWS had a large Bio-Nuclear arsenal; however satellites and radiation detectors confirmed ZERO RADIATION. No one alive on earth knew what caused the explosion, who did it and why . . . ???

A Post explosion satellite video capture survey of the location showed 2 white spots which appeared a minute after the explosion which combined and disappeared seconds later.

We all saw the satellite image on TV, there was chaos. Nothing was visit able anymore. The explosion had caused outbreaks, riots everywhere on earth. Roads were jammed, people were being massacred. No one knew what they were doing and where they were going. It seemed the fury was on peak.

With the Prevailing conditions we had to travel continuously. We were not safe outside our running cars. Our dream of a 700km picnic had been ruined. Now our only other option, aim, locus and focus and everything was to reach back to our farmhouse within the shortest time possible. No stops and maximum possible speeds were the call of the time. Travel either at day or night was a terrifying experience. We saw many slaughters and held up people as we smashed through all the barriers at top speed. There was only FEAR in our mind, the fear of the known, which was now, unknown. God! We wanted to reach home. While coming back, people tried to pull Anvesha out through the open door, Avni ran over 6 of those bastards and teared the door off my car, but thankfully we managed to escape. We had to keep hatches open to prevent drag, but on another encounter miscreants tore the hatch doors off. Anvi drove as I preferred to sit on the side without the door, with reinforced seat belts. Boulders, bottles, knives, petrol bombs had been hurled at our cars. The bonnet caught fire and the windscreen broke at a speed of135kmph; we nearly lost control and could have toppled over when a bottle was hurled at us. Avni's car tyre burst at 170kmph, she rammed into a pole which tore her car into two. Miraculously she survived, but lost her senses. We left her car to rot.

It was a time to end that all. It was now our rat race for survival in the hostile environment.

3 days later we reached our farmhouses after crossing rivers of blood, piles of dead bodies and cities resembling tanneries. These 3 days had been the worst days of our lives. We looked back at our car; the best word to describe it would be battered. Each and every glass was broken, each metal part was dented including the wheel rims, there was blood splashed over the seats, tires, engine, and the complete body. It looked more like a vehicle to hell, rather than something which brought us back home.

We walked towards our bungalows. To give a positive end to the horrifying trip, we were now accomplished in combat against savages; and could use any object lying around to protect ourselves. But home was not as we expected it, savages had reached our homes, there was blood on the walls, blood on the floor, in the garden, in the garage, the tap was oozing polluted blood water. We were scared. We raced to find our parents. My brain had now lost all sensory perception. As we reached our houses, I saw coagulated blood on the mud and water flowing over it through the gate. "Shit . . ."

There were 55 dead bodies in and outside our houses. We searched the 6 houses and all we could find was ransacked houses and a liberal spray of blood which covered everything from the god's idols to the bed sheets. The houses smelt worse than a garbage bin of slaughter house. We were terrified. We could not find our parents any where . . . All we found were the 2 burnt down cars with blood and skeletons inside them.

We went inside the last one of the houses.

"This blood seems nearly a week old." Avnika said.

"Is that so you forensic bitch?" Anvesha screamed. It was not a terrified scream and it messaged something else.

"Take hold of yourself Anvesha . . ." Anik stepped in. With fear in mind and a splitting headache now, I did not know what to say or react.

"Shut up your ass, bastard." Anvesha screamed. It was now a revenge seeking scream.

"Damn you, we all are scared. Just shut your mouth." Kelly shouted.

"Shouting at me you whore . . ." Anvesha slapped Kelly harder than a rock. Before anyone could react to that she grabbed hold of Kelly's hair and banged her head on the wall. Anik ran to Kelly as she fell down as I and Avnika looked at Anvesha in horror.

"What are you doing you asshole bitch?" Avnika shouted.

"It was your idea isn't it? Of this picnic?" Anvesha picked a knife and walked towards Avnika.

"Anvesha, you bitch, you killed her . . ." Anik rushed towards her with water pipe lying nearby. I ran to stop him and got hold of the pipe, he lost his balance and fell down; but in a flash he got up and head butted her in the stomach and banged her on the wall. Anvesha let out an ear splitting scream and plunged the whole 9 inch knife in Anik's back and spine. Anik let out a continuous soul splitting shriek as Anvesha hacked his body nearly hundred times as the knife in her hands made way from his waist to the neck. She stopped when Anik collapsed.

"Save me from this . . ." Avnika grabbed my arms in horror and stood behind me.

Anvesha was not able to walk straight due to the head butt. The knife in her hand was dripping the red thick fluid; her hair, clothes, teeth, face were covered with blood, blood and more blood. She limped towards us with rage in her eyes. She was looking horrifying, dreadful and scary. Avnika clutched me in terror. We could not run away, Anvesha was standing at the door.

"Anvesha what are you doing? Things have been very bad as it is you have made it worse." I shouted and Avnika's nails dug deeper in my skin. Anvesha walked closer.

"Don't do it." Avnika screamed and her nails pierced my skin.

"Talk to me Anvesha." I freed from Avnika and walked to Anvesha. I was scared but still I walked closer.

"Don't be a fool, she's lost it . . ." Avnika screamed and tried to pull me back. I walked towards her, she was angry but she did not harm me, I was shit scared. It was like walking to a wild animal who did not know any right or wrong. She stopped as I got closer, my heart raced like never before with fear. I reached close to her, she pulled up her knife.

"I am not going to do anything to you, what has happened to you? Can you see what have you done? You killed your friends . . ." I said.

"They were not my friends; it was due to this bitch and them both that our families were massacred." Anvesha shouted.

"Due to me damn it? What did I do?" Avnika shouted back desperately.

"This picnic was your idea you bastard." Anvesha shouted back, but she lost her balance and fell on her knees down. I went and held her.

She fell in my arms, she felt the same to hold but I did not know what had got into her. I was afraid holding her and the stench which followed made me frightened. Her hair was all sticky with blood and flesh, her complete body was covered in the blood of her friends, she looked at me with anger.

"She killed my family, that motherfucking princess." Anvesha tried to get up and move towards the scared Avnika.

"Shit . . . nooooooo." Avnika screamed.

"Anvesha, dear she hasn't done anything, please don't behave like this." I said with tears in my eyes. "I can't see you like this please become just like you were a couple of hours back please please please . . ." I cried nonstop and hugged her. My tears fell on her shoulder and washed off some of the blood and exposed her fair skin. She let go of the knife and hugged me back tight, I closed my eyes. "But that bitch killed my family." Before I could say anything Anvesha let out a blood curdling scream in my ears. With my open eyes I saw the complete knife in Anvesha's back and Avnika holding it. Anvesha's screams and tears tore through my head as I saw Avnika holding the handle.

"You asked for it bitch." Avnika said and twisted the knife.

Another horrific scream rang in my ears. Anvesha grabbed Avnika's hand and twisted it hard. Avnika screamed and fell face down on the floor.

Anvesha looked at her and me with rage and screamed, "So this was your grand plan."

Anvesha pulled her knife from Avnika's hand and in a flash of a second lodged it in the back of her neck. With a mind numbing scream Avnika died.

I tried to get up, "Where are you going you skunk bastard?" She screamed at me.

With her legs she tripped me and jumped over on my chest, "So you changed sides huh?" She said menacingly to me. Blood gushed from her back on my stomach. I was scared to hell. "I did not know she was going to do such a thing." I cried with fear.

"Well, you will not know anything now." She screamed and without a second thought plunged the knife in my throat with full force. I felt excruciating pain as it came out through the back of my neck.

Location—Bluecover Corp.

Investigations were at full throttle in the Bio-engineering and cybernetics to find out what caused the explosions which wiped out the BWS, and importantly the origin and end of the white spots on the satellite images. The success rate was however ZERO. The shiny granite only made the situation more mysterious.

Sheemal Jezebeth was however not concerned with what was happening. On the 3rd day of the takeover, under his supervision a group of Para military force with cybernetic equipment slaughtered the complete staff of BARC and the Nuclear Division of Bluecover. He ordered the secret group placed for the PM's security to be murdered along with the PM's family. The order was carried out with precision but the news leaked out with pictures and what followed were the worst 2 days of Indian history.

Monster scale massacres, riots, genocides, homicides, daylight murders, rapes, robberies etc became common place. There were 35 lakh people killed in the 35000 riots just in two days. The population was going down by volumes worldwide. Conditions in cities turned from liveable to concentration camp like in 12 hours. Thousands and thousands were being mercilessly eliminated for no fault of theirs. Satellite images of the earth no longer showed the land masses as green, they were now red, even the Sahara and Antarctica. The colour of the water was also darker, near to black rather than blue.

30 and 31st December were the worst nightmares any city could have. City streets resembled the yards of slaughter houses. The condition had degraded to the most horrendous scene in history. Bluecover Corp. had wrongly played its worst game and havoc with the most peaceful place in the universe; The EARTH.

LOCATION—Central India, 1 Jan

Rioters had split open 350,000 men and animal bodies on the road. Like cannibals they were playing with organs which had come out of the bodies as they kicked the mangled bodies inhumanly. At the present location there were 10,000 rioters who were molesting young kids on gun and knife points. The cross roads were filthy graveyards. The stench was overwhelming. It seemed that the time had come . . . for the divine to step in. Now there were 4 parts of FALSEHOOD and 0 of Truth.

The time was 12 noon and it was sunny. Suddenly the sunlight intensity started to decrease and all the activities stopped. The sky did not have any clouds or any possible obstruction to the sun. One of the loudest thunders in the history of the planet was heard which forced everybody's fingers in their ear canal. Moments later, people saw a very large cloud of dust and debris approaching them. As it came forward, it destroyed everything in its path. Trees, poles, foundations, buildings it uprooted everything. No one seemed to move in the world except the twister. Everyone saw a bright white center inside the twister which was increasing in size. As the twister approached the crossroads, it slowed down and stopped. Eyes strained to take a look at the 12 feet globe in front of them. People could only make out a face with an angry expression. A few in the mob rushed towards the figure with swords and axes, the next moment 200 lightning bolts struck around the globe reducing the attackers to pieces of burnt flesh and placed the globe at the center of a 40 feet wide elevation of granite.

The sun went out completely and at 1215hrs, it was just an aura of light on every part of the earth. The force field (white globe) seemed to disappear slowly. People could figure out 2 faces inside. **One of a human, and the other of a horse.**

Out in space, all the satellites were automatically being focussed at Central India by an unknown power. All satellites, cell phone, Wi-Fi, WI-MAX, radio, and HDTV networks were shutdown for 5 seconds and restarted. Those seemed like the longest 5 seconds in history. It seemed that the earth was being reprogrammed. Every capable device was now transmitting the voice of the man in Central Delhi.

Worldwide everyone looked at the man and his horse in awe. He had a most radiant face of all the humans born in the galaxies. He had a magnificent aura of power around him. The air surrounding him was extremely pure although no one could go near. His skin wheatish in colour had a radiance which was unseen after the start of Kali-Yug. The pure white clothes he wore had the most exquisite jewels on it, and had a glow equivalent to the sun. The horse was quantum times the best breed on the planet. It was a winged one and shoes of diamond which shone bright when he lifted his feet.

The horse jumped his front feet in the air and neighed loudly. It was louder than all the horses put together. Lakhs of people had now gathered at the site. Every display in the world from a watch to a projector was showing Central India.

Everyone soon noticed a sword by the man's waist. He threw a look on the massive mob around him. Every person had some kind of a weapon in his/her hand. They all looked at the man in white clothes with terror.

"I warned you before!" the man said in a thundering voice. His each word shook the air as he spoke them. His voice was magnetic, majestic and unavoidable. Blind men could see and the deaf could hear. The world or for the matter 'Earth' had been taken over by a super natural force, everything now seemed to be focussed on the man and his horse—Devdatta.

The man continued,

"I warned you many times! Each time you commit the same mistake, not just one, you all refuse to learn from the past. Every one of you wants to be greater than DIVINE. You forget that you are humans, you consider yourself god. Each time I think you will take a good path, you did something that was more disgraceful. Each time I made it well, you made it worse. Today the time has come when I will do it for the FINAL time . . . Brace yourselves because the end is here."

He drew out his sword. The sword glowed with a brightness equivalent to 100 suns blinding all the people who were watching him worldwide. The engraving on the sword in Sanskrit, said,

"KING OF THE KINGS, GOD OF THE GODS. HE IS THE START AND HE IS THE END"

"To all gods, this is a request; please take your feet of this filth. To the soul of the EARTH, I order you to leave the planet; this place is no more capable of holding you and purity."

All of sudden, there were millions of explosions on the planet, the flames of which reached into space. Mosques, churches, temples and homes burst into flames, all the people inside were reduced to ashes, and trillions of Euros worth of architecture collapsed in seconds. Moments later a blue fireball arose from every holy statue, photograph, locket, finger ring, and tattoo, from churches, temples and homes and some human bodies. As the fireballs rose up in the air, the statues, photographs, articles and humans turned to pieces with a blast.

Far away the Kaaba, from its centre evolved huge blue fireball. The land on which the Kaaba was standing collapsed into the unknown abyss.

All the fireballs rocketed into the atmosphere and combined into a single huge star and disappeared.

"The 7 pure souls who reside on this planet, waiting for my arrival, it is now time that you arise."

In the forests, the soul of Ashwatthama rose as a pink fireball from his ghoul body. The fireball sparkled a lot as it went above the ground and then to the feet of the man.

There was an earthquake in the region of south India, the land split into 2 and from below the abyss arose another pink fireball, the soul of Raja Bali. It dipped once and payed homage to the man.

The mountain of Chitrakoot split into 5, from between them arised the five faced fireball of Lord Hanuman which bowed down to the man.

From one of the unknown valleys of the Himalayas in Himanchal, appeared another pink fireball to which the man bowed down in respect. It was the soul of Parshurama. All the trees and vegetation turned dry as the soul left the valley.

100 tornadoes with the speed of 3000kmph destroyed the island nation of Lanka taking it completely into the ocean. As it went inside the

water it left behind a fireball which was the soul of Vibhishana.

From the deepest portion of the river Beas in Punjab, arose a fire so huge that it vaporised the whole river and from its centre arised the soul of Maharishi Ved Vyas, to which the man bowed his head down.

Dwarka in Gujarat was coming up from its underwater location, as it came up, a pink fireball; the soul of Kripacharya came out from it. It too bowed down to the man.

'Who is he?' people world over the world, had a question in their minds

"Who am I, is your last doubt, at this moment, I announce with my arrival, the arrival of the MAHA-AVTAR . . . . THE ARRIVAL OF KALKI!" he announced with a royal booming voice which shook the foundations of every structure on the earth.

"The time to make everything pure once again has come . . . ." he raised his glowing sword and pointed it to the heavens above. Over a million lightning bolts struck the sword every second. The earth shook violently and raising both his hands the lord said,

"Yada Yada Hi Dharmasya, Glanirbhavati
Bharata . . .

Abhyuthanam Adharmasya, Tadatmanam
Srujamyaham . . .

Paritranaya Sadhunaam, Vinashaya Cha
Dushkrutaam,

Dharma Saunsthapanarthaya Sambhavami
Yuge Yuge!!!"

The penultimate destruction started, the polar caps started melting at an unimaginable speed, the Svalbard Global Seed Vault was destroyed first, the oceans were rising at a speed of 100 ft per second, and the furious rising waters destroyed all the coastal cities of the world. The sun came out again, its heat and intensity increased over hundred folds and poured fire over all the inland regions burning everything in view. All the technological innovations ever sent by humans in space including the Voyager Golden Record started falling back to the earth.

The Treasure of Gods turned into a raging volcano and as it erupted, it spewed out molten gold over a radius of 3000 kilometres, all humans and animals melted into a screaming mass of red and gold as the boiling molten metal made its way through the skin, muscle and bone.

A loud screech came out of the sword, which tore the eardrums of every creature on the earth, the light emanating from the sword dried every eyeball on the planet, the complete human race tried to evade the destruction running here and there 'blind' and the chaos was at its realm. Now there was no escape . . . .

Lord KALKI waved his sword in the air sending thousands of volts in the atmosphere. Thunderstorms were being created; the hurricane on which he had arrived was now alive. He got down from his steed, and took his sword in both the hands. Everything had collapsed, the rest was going down or was about to do so . . .

He looked at the black sky above, the hurricanes were now unstoppable and had energy equivalent to a million nuclear arsenals.

With both his hands, he raised the sword in the air pointing towards the earth; the sword gleamed bright enough to make the sun look like a firefly.

"THE END IS NOW_____ . . . ." Lord KALKI shouted with all his might, blood rained from the sky, the earth stopped rotation on its axis; collapsing under its own gravity the crust broke at several places taking inside humans, animals, buildings, ships, cars and planes into the molten magma. It was the most horrendous site, which no one could witness. Anyone who could see was no longer alive. Torrents of the furious oceans sank everything that came in their way.

With all his might KALKI struck the sword into the ground and from that point, a massive wave of explosion spread forward which had more than 1000 times the energy of all the nuke in the universe put together. The wave sped at an astonishing velocity and vaporizing stone, metal, oceans, sea beds, mountains, land and destroying everything in its way in its 2 waves on the earth.

The legacy had done it, 4 parts of deception around the world had invited him. KALKI climbed onto his steed and raised his sword . . . the rains stopped . . . He looked around, what was a concrete road a few minutes ago was now barren granite.

He smiled and placed his sword back into its case. With his left hand he pulled the reign of the horse, the horse neighed loudly, fluttered its wings and raised his front legs in the air . . . .

"10 days later a new era begins . . . An era of purity and peace . . . The humans will rise again . . ." Lord KALKI announced looking at the 7 pure souls, and the earth regained its rotation.

The horse galloped at a speed greater than light and disappeared into the distant horizon . . .

THE END

—∞∞∞—

Raj took his eyes off the diary, and then looked at his GF in awe. This really was the grandest story told to him. The story, the surreal environment created, the characters, the places, all were revolving in his head. He did not know when he fell asleep. He had lost track of time and now the jet-lag was catching up with him.

Many hours later when he woke up he saw a lot of people in the room. However he was unable to grasp the things which were happening. He tried to stand but unable to keep his balance due to drowsiness he fell down, half on the couch and floor. The talks told him that GF was alive but something was wrong.

"Oh, you got up. Are you fine now?" Lina asked as she held him up.

"What happened is he fine?" Raj asked as he got up.

"Well, there's good news and bad news." Lina quipped.

"What is it?"

"He is now out of danger, but won't be able to talk or do things . . ." She said.

Raj hugged Lina tight. She could feel his warm tears and his breathing on her skin. A wave surged inside her body and her brain registered the event nearly 10 times.

"Oh, I am sorry." Raj said as he realised what he was doing, not to mention the number of eyes which were looking at them.

His father walked to them, mother followed. "Raj . . . This is not America." Mom said in the angry tone. "Cool down." Father said to mother.

"Raj you need a break, go have a coffee both of you." He said to Raj and Lina.

"But him . . ." Raj said pointing towards GF.

"He's my father Raj; I think I can handle things here." His father replied with authority and sternness in his voice which meeked Raj. "Go now." He added. Raj walked out. Lina followed him but was stopped by Raj's mom.

"Just take care of my weird son." She said to Lina.

"Don't worry." Lina smiled and said

They reached the cafeteria, had a piping hot coffee and ordered a fresh sandwich.

"How did you come here? How did you find me?"

"I tracked you . . ." She replied.

"Eh . . . ?"

"Yes." Lina said as a canteen staff came and placed 2 fresh sandwiches in front of them and walked away.

"Howww?" Raj asked, lines criss-crossing his forehead.

"After you left the airport, I got hold of the boarding passengers list, from the boarding pass number; it was easy to get to your ticket. The ticket had all the details of when, where and how you booked the ticket. With the help of a computer expert, we had your IP address, street address in New York and your credit card number."

"My credit card number????" Raj nearly squealed with horror.

"Come on dude, all these things are linked together, didn't you know?" Lina quipped matter of factly.

"No I did not . . ."

"Listen, we track each and every movement of yours on the World Wide Web, but that's not important. Then I called up on your home number."

"It was on the answering machine."

"Yes, so then what we did was to hack into the phonebook of your answering machine."

"What?? Youuuuu . . . !!"

"From the number we got, we video called your office in NY from a random American number, pretending to be your friends who wanted to give you a surprise you in India, and while the call was on . . ."

"Impossible, the company won't give you information this way."

"Not needed, because by the time the call was over, we had the complete database of the employees from the server of your company." Lina said tapping her nails on the table and moving her hair aside from her eyes.

"You hacked into the company server????????" Raj was stunned.

"It's not a big deal; we handle Guided Navigation Technologies for airplanes the whole day, for all the major airlines in the world, getting your whereabouts was just the stone on the tip of a mountain for us."

"Damn." Raj's mind was blank trying to imagine what he heard.

"I did not store the hospital address anywhere except my brain; how did you come here?"

"Don't be dumb now, I called your home number and got your location." She laughed and said.

"You can't be an airhostess, what do you do?"

Lina's facial expression changed, from funny to emotionless and dry. "Hmmmm . . . I suppose, it's time to tell you . . ."

"What do you mean?"

"See, I work in a secret department of your company-corporation, a department which keeps track of every word and movement of yours and others."

"What the_____?"

"I told you, even words." Lina sternly said.

"Ya."

"Only a few in the company and no one outside of it knows."

"Well now a lot of Indians, the people around us know it." Raj said triumphantly.

"Oh really? Take a look around." Lina said waving her hand around.

Raj looked and that made his hair stand. The whole canteen was empty, the cashier and behind the counter staff people were not to be seen, even the door was closed. He was scared.

"What do you want?"

"Nothing, I was just looking into the fact that, whether you did or did not bluff over facts to get a leave."

"And what did you find?"

"That you did have a genuine reason."

"I still don't believe in what you just said, I have never heard or seen anything like this in my company."

"Ya, that is exactly what secret means, is it not?" Lina replied and took a bite off the sandwich.

"Huh?" Raj replied and did not notice people trickling in the canteen.

"Look at this." Lina took out a hard plastic card and showed it to him. It was an identity card with details and a photograph. Raj instantly recognised the font and the logo of his company. He sunk back in his chair. His brain had now mixed up his company and Bluecover Corporation.

Raj's father walked in towards them. "Hey Lina, how's Raj now?"

"He's better now uncle." Lina replied giggling.

"She's not what you think; she's a spy from my company." Raj said and Lina burst out laughing hard and so did his father.

"He really believed all that . . . ? ha ha ha . . ." his father said to Lina.

"I think he did." Lina said, and then banged her hand on the table as she laughed.

"You believed all that? Raj, in your lingo you deserve a LOL."

"Dad she is not what she has told you she is . . ."

"You are not an airhostess?"

"I am." Lina giggled.

"No, you are a company spy."

"She's not a spy; she is Gangadhar uncle's youngest granddaughter."

"Impossible, I've never seen her around." Raj said.

"How will you? She was in UK for the past 15 years. Got it?" his father replied and Lina 'Hi'ed' Raj.

"No no, she's got my company ID, like mine, see . . ." Raj pulled out his ID.

"Raj, there's a software called Photoshop which lets you do all that, and laminate a photo paper 6-7 times and it will become harder than a credit card. Then, all I did was to cut off the transparent borders with a pair of scissors and POOF . . . A fake ID card." Lina said and placed the fake ID with her photograph on it in front of Raj.

Raj picked it up, on closer observation he found that she was telling the truth and though the card was hard, it lacked the finesse of the original. "And the empty canteen?" He asked.

"You were so lost when we came that you didn't realize that it was already empty, it is closed for half an hour, and as for the counter people, we just talked them to stay for 10 minutes." Lina hushed.

"OMG really?" Raj smiled, for the first time.

"You slept for nearly 17 hours, in that time she too read that diary. We knew your mind would be occupied with papa, to take your mind off we did this." Raj's father said.

"And we decided to do it the story style . . ." Lina chipped.

"Raj, now listen; your grand dad is alive, but he has to go one day. Don't cry and be sad in front of him. A paralytic person wants love and care. Pity and sympathy will make him hate himself all the more. Don't treat him as a liability; treat him as an asset, something you would improve upon. Tell him how much you liked his story, maybe he can't respond verbally, but his heart will; and that is what matters in this world."

A tear trickled down Lina's cheek as Raj hugged his father.

"Now go, maybe he wants to see you both . . ."

They entered the room number 10. The nurse had made his GF sit. He rolled his eyes to see Lina and Raj. He wanted to smile, but he could not.

Raj sat facing him, "It was the most amazing story you ever told, the best and worthy of the title." A tear trickled down GF's cheek. Lina was amazed.

Raj talked for 15 minutes and when he could no longer speak sense, he touched Lina's hand.

"What?" She asked.

"You know he predicted the future . . ."

"The book, you mean?"

"No."

"Then??"

Raj hugged his grandfather and said, "This was the last story he told me . . ."